BABY MAMA

FROM HELL 2

RIKENYA HUNTER

PLEASE CHECK OUT MY OTHER TITLES:

UNLUCKY IN LOVE

HUSTLE HARD

MONEY MAKE ME COME

BABY MAMA FROM HELL

Text READMOORE to 22828 to subscribe to join our mailing list!

To submit a manuscript for our review, email us at moreambiancebooks@gmail.com

Acknowledgments

First and foremost, I give my praise and thanks to God for blessing me with this talent. I'm so blessed to have found my passion. Since I was a little girl, I enjoyed writing. I used to create false news stories with my sister, Asia, and we recorded ourselves as news anchors. During the eighth grade, I started writing and keeping a journal of my daily life until I turned twenty-one years old. (I couldn't write every day after I turned twenty-one because I became a new mom and I had no time hehehe)

I dedicate this book to my fiancé Jeremy and our daughters, Jayloni, and Janai Glaspie. Y'all three are my world. Thank you, Jeremy, for always having my back and being so supportive. I love you three so much!

A huge thank you to my Auntietay, Chantay Hunter. I cannot thank you enough for all the support, encouragement and love you've given me. You have always been there for me and I love and appreciate you so much.

Thank you God mom, LaTanya McCants for always being so supportive. I love you!

To my parents Cornel and Robin, my siblings Asia and Desmond, I love you guys.

Shout-out to my good friend Jasmine Murphy, I love you, girl! Thanks for being a great friend and a true supporter of my work. I appreciate you!

To my readers that constantly reach out to me, Dayana Lopez, Pernisha Pope, Victoriaa Morales, Jessica Sean Wilson, Tootie Williams, Farrah Clark Walton, Shekie Johnson, Cara Waller, Meagan Johnson and Desiree Emory, I thank you all for the continuous support and encouragement. I appreciate you all. <3 I'm truly sorry if I've forgotten any other names. I'll make sure I get cha next time ;)

Thank you to all my supporters! For every comment, review, sharing of my link, messages and other types of feedback, I appreciate it!

Shout-out to the greatest publisher ever, Niyah Moore! I can't thank you enough for believing in me. You're such a wonderful person. I truly thank you for having me on your team. I'm living my dream and it's because of you! You work so hard and I'm so proud of you. You're truly a wonderful, humble and amazing person. You inspire me. I'm blessed to be taking this journey with you. You're the greatest!

I can't forget my wonderful pen family, Ambiance! I love y'all! You guys are amazing and are beasts with the keys and pen. I'm so proud of all of us. We're the best baby!

Big shout-out to David Weaver, Cole Hart, and the entire TBRS FAM! <3

Chapter 1

Neron

Between trying to keep my eyes on the road and searching for Kimora's rental car, I looked like I had lost my mind as I sped down the road. I prayed that she was okay and that Gabriela wasn't behind this shit. My heart pounded against my chest as if it was trying to hammer its way out. I cursed under my breath when I saw the raindrops on my window shield. I didn't let the rain slow down my driving speed though. I drove like a bat out of hell.

After driving twenty minutes, with no luck of seeing Kimora's rental car, I finally made it to the airport. I got out of my car, not caring that I was parked in the incorrect spot. Thunder roared over my head as I was pelted with rain.

"Sir, you can't park there!" shouted the security guard, but I didn't give a fuck.

I needed to make sure Kimora was okay. When I entered the cold airport, I was drenched. Chills immediately ran over my body. I shivered as I darted towards the help desk. I approached a man who looked like he was having a bad day; as if being at work was the last place he wanted to be.

"Excuse me. I need to page my girlfriend. It's an emergency and I need to make sure she's okay," I said all in one breath.

The man scrunched up his face at me as if I had two heads.

"NOW!" I yelled, causing him to jump.

"What's her name?" he asked unsurely.

"Kimora Murphy," I replied as I looked around the airport.

Before the employee could repeat her name, I spotted her. I knew that ass from the back and that bushy hair from anywhere. I darted towards Kimora.

"Kimora," I yelled.

Some people turned around and stared, but I didn't care. Kimora turned around and was surprised to see me before her.

"Neron? Baby, what's wrong? What's going on?" she asked frantically.

"Mora, I'm so glad you're okay," I sincerely said as I pulled her to my chest and wrapped my arms around her, inhaling her scent. I instantly felt relieved that she was okay.

"Neron, what's wrong?" Kimora asked again.

"I had received a block phone call that said I shouldn't have let you leave in the rental car. I thought something was going to happen to you. I tried to call you, but your phone was dead. I'm so glad you're okay baby. You have no idea how worried I was."

"Oh, my gosh! What in the world! Who do you think it was?" Kimora asked.

"My guess is as good as yours, but I feel this has Gabriela's name all over it," I responded.

Kimora shook her head, looked up at me with those beautiful brown eyes, and kissed my lips tenderly. "Well, I'm okay baby, but I really have to get going before I miss my flight," she said smiling.

"Okay, I love you. Please call me, time you land in Miami," I said.

"I love you too, handsome. I surely will," she said as she scurried off to check her bags.

I watched her strut away as I heard my license plate and model of my car being said over the intercom. They were threatening to tow my car if I didn't move it immediately. I jogged through the airport, jumped into my car, and drove off. Thoughts swirled around in my head as I tried to figure out if Gabriela had anything to do with the phone call and what her motive was. I had a feeling the craziness was far from over. For now, I was just glad that my lady was safe and I just wanted to go home and relax.

Chapter 2

Gabriela

I stepped into the shower and let the hot water massage my body. I grabbed Kimora's peach body wash and squirted a decent amount on her pouf. I proceeded to wash my body as I imagined the pouf as Neron's hands. I closed my eyes as I thought about him making love to me. I rinsed off and turned off the shower. I grabbed Neron's towel and dried off. I wiped the fogged bathroom mirror and stared at my reflection. I was a pretty woman, but for the life of me, I couldn't understand why life always gave me the short end of the stick. I was tired of always being let down or disappointed. I grew up without knowing my father, living with a verbally abusive mother and now a man that dismissed me after my mother, I fought, and I lost our child. Neron was going to take me back and love me the way I wanted him to.

After I had dried off my body, I applied some of Kimora's Bath and Body Works Japanese Cherry Blossom lotion. I sprayed some Viva La Juicy perfume behind my ears, on my wrists and on my inner thighs. I decided to keep the perfume, so I slipped it into my purse. I put on one of Neron's t-shirts and boxers. I grabbed my wine glass from off the end table and trotted back to the kitchen to refill my glass.

I sat down on the sofa and stared at my daughter's picture. She was beautiful. If Mia was the glue that held Neron and me together, then all I needed to do was get pregnant again and he would have no choice, but to come back to me. I smiled as I thought about my plan coming into motion. After finishing my glass, I walked to the kitchen, washed it and placed it back exactly where it was. Walking out of the kitchen, I saw a laptop open. Upon scanning it, I noticed that Kimora was going to be coming back in a few days. I was going to strike the night she was due back in town. She was going to see why I was the baby mama from hell. Neron was mine and I wasn't going any damn where.

I grabbed my belongings, keeping on his clothes, and dipped out of the apartment, placing his key back underneath the mat. I sucked my teeth when I noticed it was raining. I shot towards my car as if my ass was on fire. Once inside my car, I cranked the engine and drove away as if I was never in their apartment.

Chapter 3

Neron

As I turned the corner, I could've sworn that I saw Gabriela's car, but it was hard to tell with all the rain and wind battering the car window. I pulled into my apartment complex, cut off the car and prepared to dodge the rain as best as I could. I sprinted towards my front door.

I walked into my apartment and was relieved I made it home and knew Kimora was safe and sound. I took off my wet clothes and decided to take a shower. After my shower, I made a bowl of Ramen noodles. I had a habit of adding my own seasonings and hot sauce. That was the only way I ate them. I really wanted a pizza, but I wouldn't feel right making a deliveryman come out in this awful weather. I wasn't going to cook any huge meals while Kimora was out of town either, so noodles it was.

I grabbed a cold one from the fridge, flopped down on the couch in my boxers, and put my feet up on the coffee table. I turned on the television and there was breaking news about the severe thunderstorm we were having. The rain wasn't letting up anytime soon. It was expected to stick around for a few days. They were advising people to stay home and off the road. Thousands were without power. I was blessed that I didn't get into an accident while I was out searching for Kimora. I silently thanked God for watching over the both of us and I prayed that Kimora would have a safe flight.

I felt so blessed that God placed my baby Kimora back into my life. I was already counting down the days until she returned home. I needed her with me at all times. It was crazy how she made a nigga feel all giddy inside.

After I ate my noodles and downed three beers, I decided to go to bed. I had class tomorrow. I couldn't wait to graduate from barber school and start the life I had always wanted. Now that I had my woman back, I was ready to graduate, stack my coins and get this money.

*

Today was the day Kimora was coming back home. All day in class, I couldn't concentrate because she was the only thing on my mind. I had missed my woman. She had been gone for three days. Her flight was getting in around ten tonight and I was picking her up from the airport. I refused to let her drive in this weather. The rain was still

BABY MAMA FROM HELL 2

coming down pretty hard and many were still without power. The weather was nasty as fuck.

After getting home from class, showering and eating Burger King, I decided to take a short catnap before it was time to pick up Kimora. It was something about a clean body, a full belly and the sound of the rain that equaled fucking and sleeping weather. Since Kimora wasn't here, fucking was out for now, but sleep was in. I was setting my alarm on my phone when my power went out. I sucked my teeth. Luckily my phone was charged. I shook my head when I looked out the window and saw that the street and complex was completely dark. I silently hoped that it wouldn't take long for JEA to cut the electricity back on.

Chapter 4

Gabriela

I sat in my car in Neron's apartment complex as the wind howled, the thunder rumbled and the rain lashed against the car windows. I knew this would be the perfect time to sneak into Neron's house. As I was turning off my car, the whole apartment complex and street went completely dark. *The power is out!* This was perfect and way too easy.

I couldn't wait to have Neron in my presence again. The man was gorgeous. Papi was the color of the candy *Sugar Babies.* He always had a great dress code and was very cautious of his looks. He had a Steve Harvey piano-key smile that would light up any room. His hair was always short and fresh. He always rocked a fresh line up and his hair looked like Jacksonville Beach with all the waves that occupied his head. Not to mention, the man was tall, I'm talking 6'2. Not to mention, he has big feet and you know what they say about men with big feet. Lord, just thinking about this man had me feeling like I was going to pass out.

I dug into my purse and pulled out Kimora's perfume that I had stolen the other day. I quickly sprayed on a decent amount on my body. I pulled my long tresses into a bun, not wanting my hair to give my identity away. I made sure my trench coat was tied tightly and my camera was tucked away in my pocket. I grabbed my umbrella, opened the driver side door and opened the umbrella. I stepped out of the car as the rain poured down around me and the thunder and lightning put on a show. I ran towards Neron's front door in long strides, as my peep toe heels splashed in puddles. I finally made it to the hallway and dropped my umbrella, out of breath. I lifted up the welcome mat and wasn't surprised that the front door key was right where I knew it would be.

I was taking a chance by just walking into Neron's apartment without warning, but that was a risk I was willing to take. I inserted the key into the keyhole and slowly turned the knob. Surprisingly, I wasn't nervous. I was excited. Adrenaline filled my body as I thought about seeing Neron.

I walked into the apartment and as expected it was dark as hell. I had to feel around the room to guide myself. I heard Neron snoring in the bedroom and quickly untied my trench coat. I grabbed my camera from out of the pocket and tossed the coat on the sofa.

I wished Neron could see how stunning I was looking in this black sexy lace top and matching corset panties, but it was too dark since the power was out. Many have told me that I favored Adrienne Bailon because I had that New York swag, Latina accent and was fun size.

I strolled towards Neron's bedroom that he shared with Kimora. I had to use the walls as guidance since it was so dark. I couldn't see shit, but I knew that snore from anywhere. He had a horrible habit of snoring, but hearing him snore right now, was actually music to my ears. I swiftly turned on my camera and sat it up on the dresser, directly in front of the bed.

I noticed his cell phone blinking near the bed. I hurriedly snatched it up and cracked the password. He was so predictable with his passwords. It was Mia's due date. I quickly sent myself a text from his phone so I could have his number since he had blocked me from calling him and then changed his number. After I had sent the text to myself, I deleted it, so he obviously wouldn't suspect anything.

I walked back to the dresser and pressed the record button on the camera. I wasted no time as I hoped on the bed and mounted Neron's muscular and chiseled body. I leaned in as my breasts touched his bare chest and stuck my nose under his neck. He smelled damn good. I inhaled his scent. He stirred in his sleep and I began softly kissing his neck. He started moaning.

"Umm, Kimora baby," he grunted, half asleep.

I only replied, "Um hmmm" as I continued to plant kisses on my man.

I didn't give a fuck how I trapped him. He was going to be mine. He palmed my ass and I was so glad that the room was dark; otherwise he might've caught me.

I slithered down to his boxers and pulled out his erect penis. It was standing at attention. I hurriedly wrapped my mouth around his chocolate stick, secured my hand at the base, and went to work. I had to show him what he was missing. I knew Kimora couldn't suck his dick like I could. I bobbed my head up and down and took him deeper into my throat. Neron started moaning and reached for my hair, a habit he always had when he was getting good head. I quickly shooed his hands away for fear that he would obviously know the difference between Kimora and my hair.

I started gently massaging his balls as Neron moaned. I felt his dick throbbing in my mouth and knew that I was on my shit. I released him from my mouth, not wanting him to come yet. I moved my panties to the side and slide down on his dick. I shuddered once I realized that I was making love to my baby father, again. He felt amazing as I started rocking back and forth. Neron wrapped his arms around my waist and I began to ride him like I was in the Kentucky Derby. I wanted him to yearn for me the way that I ached for him.

I leaned down and placed my lips against his. He sucked on my bottom lip, just the way I liked it and I stuck my tongue into his mouth. I sat up and placed my right hand around his neck and my left hand on his chest as I rode him.

"Fuck baby," moaned Neron as he quickly came inside me.

I increased my speed as I realized that I had accomplished what I came for. I turned around in the direction of the camera and smiled. I couldn't wait to throw this shit in perfect ass Kimora's face.

"Umm," I moaned as I came squirting my womanly juices all over his dick, like a water gun.

"That's right, give it to me," Neron groaned.

I smiled hearing the sound of my baby daddy's voice.

After I had came, I got up quickly, grabbed my camera and backtracked to the living room. I heard Neron repeatedly saying, "Kimora" in the distance, but I had to quickly get out of the house before he knew it was me.

As I bent down, sliding my camera back inside my trench coat pocket, ironically, the lights cut on and we were face to face, as I stood before him in my lingerie.

"What the fuck," Neron shouted looking frantic.

"Surprise baby," I yelled, and tossed my hands up in the air with a huge smile on my face.

"Gabriela, what the fuck are you doing here man?" Neron shouted, looking around as he stuffed his limp penis back into his boxers.

"Damn, baby daddy, I missed that dick. I wanted to surprise you, so I snuck in using the spare key you left for me under the mat. I've missed you," I cooed.

I fixed my panties and proceeded to put on my trench coat.

Within a split second, Neron charged at me as if he was a lion and I was his prey. I didn't have any time to react when he pushed my body roughly against the wall. Neron had never put his hands on me before. He was furious.

"Neronnnnn," I softly spoke, trying to calm him down.

Before I could even fathom what happened, I felt a sting on my cheek. Neron had literally slapped the taste of out my mouth because spit flew from out of my lips. He was pissed. His eyes looked like they were going to pop out of his head and he was breathing so hard that he sounded like a black grizzly bear. He grabbed my shoulders and squeezed so tightly that I felt as if he was going to break a bone.

"Gabriela, It's taking every fiber in my body not to beat your ass like a nigga. I don't understand how you could think that I want you! I ain't been sending any fuckin' missed signals. I don't love you. I never loved you. I've moved on. We are done. Done!" Neron shouted so loud that I was sure the whole block could hear him.

"I'm sorry baby, but I miss you so much. I need you in my life. I can't function without you. Besides my brothers, you're all that I have," I sobbed.

WHAP!

Neron had slapped me again. The smack brought more tears to my eyes and they began to cloud my vision.

"Cut the bullshit. You're fuckin' crazy! I swear you're the baby mama from hell! Are you that pressed for dick, that you'd sneak into my shit and fuck me? You're doing any and everything to try and break Kimora and me up, but that won't happen. Get your shit and get the fuck out of my house before I retract my statement and you become the first female I ever beat down," Neron shouted.

At this point, I was crying hysterically and snot was running from my nose. I just wanted him to hold me, tell me that he loved me and really cared for me. I wanted to speak and try to defend myself, but I knew he meant business. I definitely fucked up this time. I saw the rage in

23

his eyes. He already slapped me, not once, but twice, so I knew he wasn't lying.

After he had released his grip on me, I snatched my car keys from off the sofa as Neron opened the front door. As I was walking towards the door, he forcefully pushed me out the door that I fell and scraped my knee on the concrete. I cringed in pain as I grabbed my knee. I jumped when I heard him slam the door behind me.

"Fuck you Neron! Fuck you!" I shouted, pissed off that he had yet rejected me again.

No, I didn't mean that! I love him! I'll never stop loving him.

I got up from the ground and dusted myself off. I silently cried as I eyed my scraped and bleeding knee. I glanced at my umbrella and decided to leave it. I limped back towards my car as I pulled my car keys from out of my trench coat pocket. I didn't care that I was getting rained on. I turned around in the direction of Neron's apartment, hoping that he was going to come chasing after me and confess his love for me. I must've stood in the rain for thirty seconds, just waiting for Neron to come running out the door, but he never did.

I sat in my car and cried like a newborn baby. My mascara had a race with my tears as it ran down my cheek and fell on my chest. This man doesn't love me. If he did, he would be ruining my lipstick with his kisses and not ruining my mascara from making me cry. I wiped the snot from my nose on the back of my hand and remembered the sex tape I made without Neron's knowledge.

Maybe I still do have the upper hand in this after all. He's going to regret ever rejecting me.

Chapter 5

Neron

"Fuck!" I yelled at no one in particular as I slammed the front door.

I was so angry. It took everything in me not to lay hands on Gabriela's stupid ass. My parents didn't raise me to hit women and although I felt bad about slapping Gaby, she deserved that shit.

I couldn't believe her! My heart was racing, sweat poured down my face and my hands trembled. I stood looking at the spare key that she had placed on the coffee table. This bitch really broke into my house and fucked me! I bawled my fist up and stopped myself from punching the wall. I wouldn't know how to explain the dent to Kimora. Another man might've dreamed about getting fucked by surprise, but not me. I was going to lose Kimora. There was no way possible she would believe me if I told her this shit. This couldn't be happening to me.

My alarmed kept chiming on my cell phone, alerting me that it was time for me to get up and pick Kimora up from the airport. Her flight would be landing in about an hour. I walked to the bedroom and shut off the alarm on my phone. All of a sudden, I wasn't ready to see Kimora. I didn't want to see the look of hurt or disappointment on her face. I didn't do anything wrong, so why did a nigga feel guilty as hell?

I decided to shower, to wash Gabriela off of me. I was half-asleep and it was dark as hell, I couldn't tell that it was her fuckin' me. Obviously I assumed that Kimora came home early to surprise a nigga. I even smelled her favorite perfume. I would've never guessed that Gabriela snuck into my house to have sex with a nigga. Damn man.

The first thing that came to my mind was me hitting her raw. It was one thing that I was tapping Kimora unprotected, but to do it with Gabriela and unwillingly is an entire different story.

"Lord, please don't let her crazy ass get pregnant," I said to myself as I continued to scrub myself clean.

After my shower, I tossed on some red basketball shorts and a wife-beater tank. I sprayed on Blue Jeans by Versace Cologne, grabbed my 14k rope chain from off the dresser, and placed it over my head and around my neck. I slid on my black Jordan slides and was ready to bounce.

I sat in the car fumbling through my CD case. I needed some shit I could ride to that would calm me down because I felt Kimora wasn't going to forgive me for this mess with Gabriela even though I had nothing to do with it.

I found a mixed Rick Ross CD and inserted it into the CD player. I cranked the car up and drove out of my parking spot as I listened to Ricky Rozay ease my mind.

Chapter 6

Kimora

As the airplane landed, I silently thanked God for letting us land safely in this weather. We had some turbulence but, all in all, I was so happy to have my feet on the ground again. I couldn't wait to see my man. I had missed him so much.

I quickly scurried to baggage claim, as I powered on my cell phone and sent Neron a quick text message saying I arrived and safely landed. I waited for my bags as I put all my weight on my right leg. I was growing impatient and couldn't wait to see my baby. I looked down at my Michael Kors watch and read the time.

"Excuse me miss."

I turned around and saw a tall, dark and handsome man before me. I know it sounds cliché, but the man was FINE! As fine as he was, he wasn't shit compared to my Neron. He favored Terry Crews, you know the father from Everybody Hates Chris.

"Yes," I replied.

"Your bracelet must've fallen off. Here," he replied as he bent down and picked up my bracelet. He passed me my bangle and smiled. I noticed that he had a beautiful set of teeth.

"Wow, thank you! I didn't even realize that it fell off," I responded as I placed the bracelet back on my wrist.

"My pleasure beautiful, miss...."

"Kimora," I said, turning back around and eyeing the bags circling the baggage claim conveyer belt. I had yet to see my luggage and was growing very intolerant.

Now, I had to admit that I was looking flawless. Of course, I had to look extra good for my man. I had been away for a few days, so I had to make sure I arrived irresistible and on point. I was rocking Blac Chyna's 88 Fin line. I was filling out a hot pink two-piece tank top and knee length skirt set. To finish off my look, I wore some closed beige heels. My natural Tracee Ross hair was dyed period red and I looked damn good.

"Well beautiful, my name is Jamie. I would love to call you sometime. Could I possibly get your number?" The unknown guy asked as I turned back around to face him.

"I'm sorry. I'm in a relationship and…"

Before I could even finish my sentence, Neron rolled up on us and went off!

"Yo, she's taken nigga. Step off!" he shouted as patrons looked on, pointed and whispered.

Jamie looked at Neron as if he wanted to get buck and I prayed that this didn't get physical.

"Man, I'm sorry. I didn't even get to ask if she was taken bruh. I just saw her bracelet on the floor, handed it to her and complimented her. My bad," Jamie said as he held up his hands in surrender and walked off.

"Neron, what in the world is wrong with you?" I asked as I spotted my bags coming my way.

"I should be asking you, what is wrong with you! You in here flirting with this man, giving him the impression that you're single," he said, a little too loudly for my liking.

I ignored him and walked towards my bags. I went to reach for my luggage when Neron slightly bumped me and grabbed my luggage before I could. I sucked my teeth as he walked towards the exit, not even bothering to apologize or wait up for me.

I was instantly pissed off at Neron. What in the hell was wrong with him? He's never acted like this before. I scurried behind him as fast as I could in my four-inch heels. I walked through the sliding glass exit doors and saw him placing my bags into the back seat. He didn't even bother to open my door. I shook my head as I saw him get into the car and slam the door shut. I opened the passenger side door and slid inside.

"What the fuck is your problem Neron?" I barked as I folded my arms across my chest and glared at him.

"You flirting with that clown ass nigga like you ain't taken," he said as he pulled into oncoming traffic.

"I wasn't flirting, Neron. He found my bracelet and gave it to me. That was it. It was barely a conversation between the two of us. Why in the world are you tripping? Last time I checked, you betrayed me!" I yelled.

I hated playing that card, but it was the truth. Why in the hell was he jumping down my throat when I had been faithful to him since day one? Last time I checked, I've never fucked any of his friends nor gotten pregnant by any of them. He had one more time to come at me and I was going to set his ass straight as an arrow.

There was complete silence. The only thing that could be heard was my breathing and the sound of the rain. I looked out the window and took a deep breath. I was so anxious and excited to see him and he ruined it.

"I'm sorry," Neron said.

"What's wrong? Why are you so angry and lashing out?" I asked, turning my attention back towards him.

"I just had a rough day. I'm sorry baby," he replied.

"Well, I'm sorry you had a rough day, but you know you can always talk to me. I'm a good listener," I said as I placed my hand on his thigh.

"Thanks, baby. It was just a rough day at school, that's all. I'm just ready to finish baby. I shouldn't have snapped at you."

"It's okay," I said seductively as I licked my lips. I started to slide my hand down his shorts to unleash his baby maker when he lightly grabbed my hand.

"Not now Mora baby," he simply said.

"Not now," I said raising an eyebrow.

"You never turn down kinky car head," I said surprised.

"I just have a headache and I'm tired baby. Plus, you know how good your head is and I gotta concentrate on the road with this weather," he said smirking at me.

"Okay, I'll get you right when we get home then," I replied.

"We'll see, baby."

I don't know what is going on with him, but I'm surely going to find out. He didn't utter another word after that. He didn't even notice that I had a new hairstyle. My hair was red like a fire truck and he didn't even notice. How could he miss that? Hell, he didn't even ask me about my trip or how Kennard, my stepmother or my father were doing. This was so unlike him. Something was bothering him and knowing Neron, he would tell me soon, on his own time.

Chapter 7

Neron

We made it back home from the airport and the rain was finally starting to slack up. It was just sprinkling. I cut the car off and before Kimora could hop out the car, I stopped her. I felt terrible being mean to her. I didn't mean to come off that way. With the shit that happened with Gaby, and then seeing Kimora talking to another man, it made me feel insecure, guilty and jealous. I was wrong. I can admit that.

"I'm really sorry Kimora for acting like an ass. I will never, ever, act that way again. You forgive me, baby?" I said sincerely.

"You know I forgive you," Kimora said with a smile.

I got out of the car and walked around to open the passenger door. She slid out of the seat and leaned in to kiss me. Her lips felt like heaven against mine. They were so soft that they felt like cotton.

"You know you look bad as hell baby. I love that hair color too," I said smiling.

"You noticed," she said surprised, smiling.

"How could I miss that loud ass hair color," I joked as we busted out laughing and walked towards our apartment.

"Whose umbrella is this?" Kimora asked.

FUCK! I didn't even notice the umbrella when I left to pick up Kimora. Think. Think!

"It's probably one of the neighbors. The wind was blowing hard as hell earlier. It might've just blown this way and landed in front of our door."

"Oh," Kimora simply said as I unlocked the door and we walked into our apartment.

Kimora sighed and flopped down on the sofa and took off her heels.

"Oooh, it feels good to be home," she said yawning.

"You know what to do, put those crusty feet on me," I said sitting down beside her.

"Shut up! You tried it," she replied laughing so hard that she snorted.

Kimora placed her legs on my lap and I started gently massaging her feet. She closed her eyes and leaned her head back on the armrest and we talked about her trip and how the family was doing back home. Her father was still going to pay her regular salary for six months, so she was going to enjoy her time off. However, she had mentioned that she was thinking of opening up a sub realty company here in Jacksonville. She was going to mention it to Dewayne really soon to see what he thought about the idea. My baby always had a plan in motion, beauty and brains.

"Mmm, that feels so good baby. You have magic hands."

"You know I can make other things feel good too," I said smirking and licking my lips.

Kimora lifted her head and started laughing and calling me nasty, but she got her behind up and walked towards our bedroom though. I followed behind her as I smacked her ass one good time. She giggled.

Once in the bedroom, I wrapped my arms around her waist from behind and planted kisses on her neck. She turned around and we locked lips, tasting each other's tongues.

"Take this shit off," I simply said.

I watched Kimora slowly shed her clothes until she stood before me, naked. I quickly undressed as she slowly crawled on the bed. I watched her toot her ass up in the air in the doggy style position. I smiled at the sight of her apple shaped ass as I stroked my dick. I got on the bed and stuffed my face in her sweet center. She tasted so sweet that I felt like I was eating a peach.

"Mmm, Neronnnnn," Kimora moaned as she buried her face into the sheets and reached underneath her to massage my balls.

"Keep doing that shit," I mumbled.

I gently slid two fingers inside her as I continued to feast on her forbidden fruit like Pac-man. When I felt her shake, I slide inside her and slowly stroked her. I could stay inside her forever.

"Damn girl, you feel so good. I missed this shit," I grunted.

"I missed you too baby. Go faster!"

I sped up and hit all her spots like ping pong as I groped her breasts. She felt so good that I was ready for her to get hers because I couldn't hold out much longer. I used to be able to go for hours, but when it came to us making love, Kimora made me her bitch.

"I love you girl."

"I love you too baby. Ahhh, I'm coming," she shouted. I continued to pound her as our headboard made its own rhythm from constantly banging against the wall.

"Shit, me too. Ugh," I roared as I sprayed her insides.

We collapsed on the bed as I pulled her body to me.

"I love you Kimora. I thank you for giving me another chance," I said feeling guilty about the Gaby incident.

Kimora turned around and looked me in the eyes.

"You know you can always talk to me and tell me anything baby. I love you too," she said as she kissed my lips. I knew she was ready for round two and I was about to give her just that until her phone rang.

"Let me see who this is, it might be daddy calling to make sure I landed safely. I forgot to call him." I watched her jump out of bed and jog out the room as her breasts bounced up and down. I smiled, feeling blessed to have her back into my life. I didn't know what to do about this Gabriela situation. There was no way that she was going to believe me. It sounded too damn crazy. Hell, I still couldn't believe it myself. I just don't want to lose her again. I felt torn. I didn't want to keep this secret from her, but I also didn't want to lose her. Fuck!

"Oh my God! Are you serious right now? Really?"

I heard Kimora shouting in the living room and instantly thought she had found out. I quickly hopped out of bed and almost busted my ass. I darted in the living room. Kimora was sitting naked on the couch and in tears as her cell phone sat beside her.

Oh my God, she knows. Damn! I should've told her. I knew Gabriela was going to run her mouth because she takes satisfaction in this drama shit.

"Mora, baby what's wrong?" I asked, scared of what she might say.

"It's my Mom; she's out of a coma! Isn't God good! They told me I could come visit her in an hour or so. I'm just so relieved. I really thought I'd lost her," she said with tears running down her face.

"Come here," I said holding my hand out for her.

I pulled her to me and hugged her tightly as she shed happy tears. I was relieved that it wasn't Gabriela on the phone but overjoyed that her mother is pulling through.

"I'm going to shower and go to the hospital to see her," she said kissing me on the cheek.

"I'm going too and afterward, we can go to dinner. This is a celebration."

Chapter 8

Gabriela

I just made it home and I couldn't believe how Neron reacted towards me. I sat on the toilet seat lid in my bathroom and applied peroxide and Neosporin to my scraped and bleeding knee. I shook my head. Neron had never put his hands on me before. A tear slipped from my eye as I thought about all the good times we shared. I stood up and walked into my bedroom. I pulled the camera out of my trench coat pocket and pressed play. I intensely watched the recorded video of Neron and me making love. Just seeing how much he enjoyed it, turned me on. What I wouldn't give to relive that moment. It's a good thing I have it on tape. I must've watched it fifteen times before I reached into my nightstand and grabbed my favorite sex toy. I took my time pleasuring myself as I watched the video of Neron and me. I was going to make sure Kimora saw this video. Even if he was done with me, I was going to make sure our secret got exposed.

*

I had been putting in some applications for a customer service job and was surprised when I finally got a call back a few days ago. The position was for a collections representative. I still had my mother's bills to pay and my brothers to clothe and feed. I was going to lose them if I didn't get some type of income coming in, so I was ecstatic when I got the call back. I was starting immediately, today to be exact.

I felt like I was fifty years old, cleaning, cooking and taking care of my little brothers, but I refused to let them go into foster care. My family on my mother's side wasn't shit, so I definitely had to start stacking some coins.

"How do I look?" I asked my brothers.

"You look nice sis," they said in unison.

"Thanks," I said smiling.

I was wearing a black DOTS pencil skirt that stopped slightly above the knee. I paired the skirt with a basic black and white striped blouse and some black three-inch peep toe heels. My hair was pulled into a neat bun with a strand of hair curled on each side of my face. I was nervous as if it was the first day of school.

I walked towards the kitchen and pulled out the boys' lunches and we headed out the door so I could drop them off at school. I couldn't be late on my first day.

I hadn't spied or attempted to contact Neron in a few days. I needed to recollect my thoughts before I pulled my next trick. He was really upset with me, but he was going to regret every single harsh word that he hurled at me. I still was in love with him, but I wanted him to hurt since he constantly kept hurting me. I had to push Neron to the back of my mind though and concentrate on my first day of work.

*

After dropping off the boys at school, I made the ten-minute drive to my new job. My stomach was doing cartwheels and I had gas like crazy. The boys were so happy when I dropped them off at school because I was lighting up the car. I've never had a job before so I was nervous about what to expect.

I turned off the engine and pulled down my visor to double check my makeup. After being satisfied with my look, I stepped out of the car and walked towards the entrance. The building was huge with too many windows to count. There were so many females at this job that I knew it was nothing, but gossip and drama going on around here.

I walked inside the building and was instantly greeted with the cold A.C. I instantly thought about bringing a jacket or sweater tomorrow because I wasn't built for the cold. I walked towards the security desk and showed him my badge that I received yesterday after orientation. He nodded and I walked towards the elevator and pressed three.

"First day?"

I looked next to me and saw a female about 5'9 with black faux locs. She had the skin of an almond with high cheekbones and a stud ring in her nose. She was sporting a red pants suit that accentuated her curves. Her body would remind you of the rapper, Fabulous' woman, Emily.

"First day?" She asked again. I was too busy looking her up and down to hear her the first time.

"Um yes, it's my first day. I'm actually quite nervous," I said as the elevator dinged and the doors opened. I watched as she walked into the elevator before me and she had a lot of juice in her caboose. Her ass was fat! I walked in behind her and we stood side by side.

"Well, you'll like it here, as long as you stay to yourself. I've been working here for almost seven months and these bitches up in here gossip and keep drama going on 'round here." Two females turned around and glanced at her, but she didn't give a damn. She kept on talking. "So, make your coins and stay to yourself," she said with a smile.

"Thanks for the heads up. My name is Gabriela by the way."

"I'm Renee. It's nice to meet you."

We smiled, the elevator door opened, and we walked through the double doors and into the office. There were about sixty cubicles and nothing, but females were occupied by all of them.

"Good morning, Miss Hernandez," said Chandra, my boss. Chandra was cool as hell, but she was business first. She was standing at 5'3 and was yellow as the sun. She rocked a wrap that stopped in the middle of her back. She dressed like Clair Huxtable and carried herself well.

"Good morning," I said with a smile.

"Ironic that you and Miss Simms are walking in together, your desk is right next to her. Renee, show her all the ropes. She had an orientation, but today is her first day. Help her feel welcomed, please."

"I gotcha boss lady," replied Renee.

Chandra winked at us and sashayed towards her office.

*

The first few hours flew by that I was surprised that it was lunchtime already. I actually did really well for my first day. Some callers were so frustrated and sounded like they needed to get laid or something. I wanted to scream, "pay your bills on time and I wouldn't have to call your ass," but I knew I couldn't say that. Not if I wanted to keep my job.

"You ready for lunch?" Renee asked, snapping me out of my thoughts.

"Yeah, I'm starving," I replied as I logged off the computer and grabbed my purse.

We walked into the cafeteria and if felt like high school all over again.

"The food is pretty good here. I'm getting a BLT sandwich."

I followed behind Renee and glanced at some of the food. I decided to have what she was having. After we paid for our subs and sodas, we found an empty table and sat down. I silently prayed over my food and looked up to seeing Renee opening her soda can.

"So, how do you like it so far?" She asked.

"It's okay. I can't really complain," I replied.

"Yeah, it's cool working here. The pay is nice," Renee said.

Renee and I sat on our hour lunch break and talked about any and everything. She was cool as hell. She was originally born in Annapolis, Maryland but moved to Jacksonville seven years ago to leave her abusive ex-boyfriend. She had no kids and she lived alone.

"So, what's your story," asked Renee in between chews. She didn't even bother to cover her mouth. Home girl spoke every time with a mouth full of food and burped every time she drunk some of her soda. She truly didn't give a fuck.

"Um, well, I have three brothers that I take care of. They're six, nine and thirteen. I don't really mess with my mother. She's in jail. She caused me to lose my daughter," I said as I suddenly lost my appetite.

"Oh damn. I'm sorry to hear that. What did she do?"

"We fought. She fought me like a bitch on the street," I said bluntly.

"Damn, that's fucked up. Well, are you still seeing your baby daddy," she said wiping her hands on a napkin.

"We're on a break right now, but that don't mean shit. So, I guess you can say we're still together. You know how that break up to make up shit goes." Renee nodded her head in agreement and I kept talking. "In fact, we're trying to have another baby right now," I said proudly. I pulled out my cell phone and showed her my screensaver, which was an old photo of Neron and me.

"That's what's up. He's cute girl. I know he'll be thrilled when you do get pregnant again," she said standing up, as lunch was over.

"Yeah, he will be," I mumbled, grinning.

*

I've been working at my job for almost four weeks and money was finally coming in. The boys were so happy to have new clothes again finally. My six-year-old brother, Mario, was constantly being teased about his shoes having holes in them. The soles were falling apart and my mother was duct taping them, to hold it together. I felt proud being able to do something nice for my brothers for a change.

Since it was Friday, I decided to have a night out with my girl Renee. Jose was thirteen years old and mature enough to stay home alone, so I left him in charge of watching the boys.

"Now, I ordered you guys three medium pizzas and I left ten dollars for an emergency. An emergency, Jose! I'm going to need that ten back if all goes well," I said, grabbing my keys and smirking at him.

He smiled and nodded his head okay. After saying goodbye to the boys, I was off to Renee's apartment.

Renee and I have been hanging out so much lately, that Neron had been slipping my mind. Maybe I should leave his ass alone and move on. Nah. Who was I kidding? That man had my heart. I decided that tomorrow, I would start putting my plan back into motion.

I had just arrived at Renee's condominium and she lived in a quiet neighborhood in Mandarin. I was wearing black leggings with a long white V-neck shirt and gold flats. I had my signature red lipstick and took the time to curl my long tresses. I felt comfortable, yet girly. Besides, we were just chilling together anyway.

I knocked on her front door and Renee quickly answered the door. She definitely looked chilled in some hip hugging tight denim shorts, a red spaghetti strap shirt, and black house slippers with a silver ankle bracelet. Her Faux Locs were tied into a ponytail and she had no makeup on her face. In her hand, I'm assuming was a glass of liquor.

"Hey girl," we said in unison as we hugged. She stepped to the side and allowed me to enter her place.

"Nice place!" I said as I looked around, checking out her spot. She had everything so organized and clean that I could eat off her floor! She had a gray and black leather-like sofa and loveseat with a black coffee table finished off with a glass top with matching end tables. Directly in front of the sofa was a thirty-two-inch flat screen.

"Thanks, you know my favorite color is black so it's only right that my living room be decorated in that color," she said smiling as she walked off towards the kitchen. I closed the front door, placed my purse on her coffee table, and sat down.

"Here girl, this shit is fiyah!" Renee spat as she handed me a glass.

"Thanks. It looks good. What is it?" I asked.

"It's a strawberry coconut daiquiri. I made a big batch too."

I took a gulp and the drink was so good that I was drinking them like a slushy. Within twenty minutes, I was on cup four. Renee and I were getting fucked up as we watched Aries Spears on Shaq's, All Star Comedy Jam. Every time I got drunk, I laughed at any and everything. I was having a good time until Renee asked me some dumb shit.

"I got some niggas about to come through, do you mind? He has a friend and they're brothers and both fine as hell," she said excitedly.

"Well, Renee, you know my baby daddy and I are trying to work things out, so as long as he's not looking for some booty to tap, we can chill out. Plus, you don't need my permission, this is your house," I said sternly. I was faithful to Neron and I wasn't about to cheat on him.

"Okay, I got chu girl. I just wanted to make sure you would be comfortable. Let me text they fine asses so they can come through," she said getting up and walking towards the back, I guess to find her cell phone to text the men.

After she had called them to come through, we had one more drink and the doorbell rang. I wasn't looking forward to chilling with some strange man. Right off the bat, I could tell how fast Renee was. Every day at lunch, she was talking about a new dude she was fuckin' heavy with.

I stood up as Renee answered the door and I wanted to smack the shit out of Renee. One dude was fine as hell. He had honey colored skin, a bald head and the biggest dimple in his left cheek. He had the type of eyebrows that had lines cut through them. He also had a top and bottom gold grill and was dressed to impress. He gave off the impression of Pete from the movie Baby Boy. He oozed money and definitely looked like he was about that life.

Now, when I looked at his brother, he looked like a square ass Cuba Gooding Jr. Now, he was handsome, don't' get me wrong, but he didn't have shit on his brother. I liked guys with a bad boy image and this guy definitely wasn't doing it for me. I wasn't looking for a quick fuck or anything, but it would've been nice if he had the same sexiness as his brother since I had to chill with him. He had no grill or any jewelry and looked like he watched porn every night because he was lonely as hell. I was livid that I would have to talk to him and entertain him while Renee got her back cracked.

"What's up ladies," said the Pete lookalike.

"We brought two bottles of Ciroc and some fye weed," said the Cuba Gooding Jr. wannabe.

"What's good," I said dryly as I sat back down on the sofa, uninterested.

"Gaby, this is Paul," she said pointing to the thug life sexy one.

"Hey," I said with a sexy smile.

"Nice to meet you beautiful," he said grabbing my wrist and kissing the back of my hand. I rose my eyebrow, looked at Renee and she was unbothered as she smiled and turned her attention to his brother.

"This is my boo, Jordon," she said, kissing the lame one on the lips.

I was so damn shocked and surprised that she was fuckin' with him instead of Paul. I automatically assumed she was messing with Paul because she told me that she usually goes for the bad boy type. I guess there's an exception to every rule. Maybe the nigga had a big dick or something because he just didn't do it for me. Now, looking at Paul as he smiled and his gold grill beamed, had my panties wet, but I needed to remain focused. I was with Neron.

Renee quickly pulled Ricardo's hand towards her bedroom as he carried a bottle of Ciroc in the other. I knew what they were about to do. I suddenly felt awkward.

"So, what's your name?"

"Gabriela, but everybody usually calls me Gaby," I said blushing.

"Okay, beautiful Gaby. Would you like a drink?" I replied yes. "I'll make you a drink. Just don't jet out on a nigga and leave a glass slipper or some shit behind," he said smirking.

"Nah, I'm not going to leave you. I promised my girl I would chill with you," I said slightly raising my voice to make sure he heard me from the kitchen.

Paul returned with two cold glasses of Ciroc and a rolled blunt. We sat talking for about an hour, laughing, drinking and smoking. I found out that Paul was twenty-eight with no kids; he had his own spot and surprisingly had two jobs; a chef and he worked cleaning carpets. He was a hustler though and that was definitely sexy. I pegged him to be a drug dealer or something and it was wrong of me to judge him like that.

I had the stamina of a horse when I drunk, but the drinks were quickly sneaking up on me, so I knew I had reached my limit.

"You want another," asked Paul as he licked his lips.

"Nah, no thanks, I'm at my limit. I was already drinking before you and your brother got here," I said politely.

"Cool. I respect that. I respect a woman that can hold her liquor. That's sexy," Paul said as he scooted closer to me. I rubbed the side of my neck in nervousness and inched away from him.

"Damn, why you running from me baby?" He asked.

"I have a man, well, we're on a break right now, but I'm loyal to him," I said matter-of-factly.

"I won't tell if you won't. Besides, your man doesn't let you have any friends?"

"Y'all niggas are funny. Why every time a female say she has a man, you guys ask can she have friends?" I said laughing.

"It was just a question baby," he said scooting closer to me.

I stood up. Okay, I'ma need you to step back and give me some space," I said firmly.

Paul stood up and rubbed his hands together. "Why, I make you nervous or something?" I looked down at the floor as we heard Renee moaning and groaning in the back room. He stepped so close to me that I felt his breath on my face. It suddenly hit me how good it felt to have someone pursue and want me. It felt good to be wanted again. I'd missed that.

He lifted up my chin and planted his velvet smooth lips on mine. It felt so good. I hadn't had a man kiss me in a while. I pushed him down on the sofa and straddled his lap. He wrapped his tattooed arms around my waist as we made out like teenagers. He was definitely a good kisser.

We broke apart from our kiss as Paul stared in my eyes.

"Renee wasn't lying when she said how beautiful you are," he said licking his lips again.

"Thanks," I said blushing.

I hopped off Paul's lap and sat beside him. "What's on your mind? I'm a good ass listener."

I twiddled my thumbs and debated if I should tell him my story. I wasn't going to tell him everything, but I most certainly would tell him about Neron kicking me, leaving me for my best friend, and how I lost my daughter. I wanted him to feel sorry for me. Everyone had looked at Neron as if he was the only victim. All life had dealt me was a bad hand at life. I never had anything go my way. It was as if the universe had it out for me. I decided to tell him part of my story.

"Wow, damn baby doll, I'm sorry to hear that. Real talk, I would've never put you out if you were carrying my baby, regardless," Paul said, wrapping his arm around my neck and pulling me closer to him when he saw a tear slide from my cheek. I inhaled his cologne and instantly felt safe and calm.

"Do you have any kids?" I asked.

"I don't have any. I ain't ready," he replied.

"Yeah, I feel you. It's hard work, but it's rewarding and such a blessing. Since the shit that happened with my mother, I'm now the guardian of my three brothers that I take care of full time."

"Damn, it seems like you got a lot on your plate. What I don't understand is why you chasing after someone you call your *man* when the nigga put you out. Why do you still wanna be with him?"

"I'm confused. He's all I've known that acted like he actually loved me besides my brothers. I'm still in love with him though and it's hard to let him go." I mumbled.

"Nah, that isn't love. From what you're telling me, he had love for you, but baby, he didn't love you. I don't respect dude for putting you out while you were pregnant, but I do respect him for being honest with you. Honesty is always the best policy. Don't fault him for being honest. Let that nigga move on and don't look back," Paul responded.

"I hate being alone. I'm not built for being single," I said crying.

Paul delicately wiped off my tears and kissed me again.

"You don't have to be alone and you don't have to settle. I'm feeling you real heavy. Let me take you out sometime. We vibin' real hard Shorty," he said as we broke our kiss.

"I would love that," I replied as Renee and Ricardo finally emerged from the room.

"Well, well, well, look at y'all two getting acquainted," said Renee. She was so drunk and high. I could tell Ricardo had put it on her. She was spent!

"Yeah, your girl is cool. I'm glad I decided to come through," said Paul. I smiled, happy that he was enjoying my presence.

I stayed for another hour as we watched Kat Williams. Renee and Ricardo had passed out and I decided to head home. Paul walked me to my car like a gentleman and we exchanged numbers. He kissed me on the cheek and told me to text him when I made it home safely. I smiled the entire drive home thinking about Paul. I was excited to go on this date with him. He definitely made some sense when he was referring to Neron. He didn't love me. Maybe I should just let him go and see where Paul and I went from here.

Chapter 9

Kimora

I was thrilled to know that my mother was out of a coma. It felt like a second chance at being able to rekindle our relationship. I didn't want to call daddy or Kennard just yet. I would give them a call after I seen her.

I wore some black denim jeans with a graphic tee and a pair of Jordan's. Neron had thrown on some beige slacks with a white tee and some black and white Jordan's. We were dressed in under ten minutes after our shower together.

*

We made it quickly to the hospital, parked Neron's car and checked in at the front desk. The polite and bubbly receptionist gave us name tags and Mama's room number. I was excited but felt jittery. Neron held my hand as we reached her room. I took a deep breath and pushed the door open. There was my mother, sipping on a cup of water. The machines next to her slowly beeped and she had no idea that we were standing there because she was watching a soap opera on the small television.

"Mom," I said softly.

"Oh my word, Kimora baby, come here," Mama replied as she smiled and sat her cup down on her tray.

My mother still looked pretty frail and her hair was in disarray yet her smile made her so beautiful at that moment. Neron dropped my hand as I slowly walked towards her bed. I leaned into her embrace and we held each other for literally a minute, not saying a word. I thought my mom was going to die, so to have her in my arms immediately started the water works.

We broke our hug and she kissed me on the cheek.

"Baby, we're going to do better and we're going to work on our relationship. This is God giving me a second chance at making things right," she said slowly and weakly.

"I truly believe that," I replied smiling.

Mom peeked around me and saw Neron standing there. Mom never really got to know him because she was always running in and out of the house, chasing men.

BABY MAMA FROM HELL 2

"Mom, this is Neron. This was someone I dated for quite a while back in high school. We reconnected and are back together. He's a great guy," I said smiling back and forth at Mama and Neron.

"Hi Ms. Roxy, it's nice to finally meet you," said Neron with a pleasant smile.

"Nice to meet you, baby. I guess you two are really serious because Mora has never introduced me to any of her boyfriends."

I tried not to roll my eyes. Neron had been my only boyfriend and I never introduced her to Neron because she was never home. Neron knew all about my mom's ways back in high school, so I knew he knew my mom was fronting and trying to act like she was the mother of the century. I know no mother is perfect, but my mom was acting as if she was. I bit my tongue and kept a smile on my face. I wanted this to be a new beginning for us.

Neron walked up to her and lightly hugged her; she accepted and hugged him back.

"How's Kennard?" She asked as I adjusted her pillows.

"He's doing fine. He's back in Miami," I replied.

I noticed my mom's jaw tightened. I guess it made her remember how dad moved us away from her. A decision I would forever be grateful for.

"Well, when you talk to him, tell him I would love to see him," she said.

"I will. So, how was the surgery?"

"Well, according to my doctors, it looks as if I'm cancer free! To God be the glory," my mom said, slightly raising her voice.

I threw my hand up in the air and silently thanked God for sparing my mother's life as tears rolled down my face. I prayed that God would bless our relationship and we could become closer as mother and daughter.

Neron and I stayed and talked to Mama for about an hour. After we had left, I called Daddy and told him the good news. He was, of course, happy and would tell Kennard the great news.

Neron and I decided to just grab some Popeye's chicken, a few Red Box movies and chill in the house. Today was a great day. I haven't been this happy in a long time. I got my man back and my mother. Things were really looking up.

Chapter 10

Gabriela

It was break time at work and Renee and I was having lunch together. I was anxious because tonight was the night I was going on a date with Paul. I was a ball of nerves. He and I had been talking for a straight week since we last met at Renee's house.

"You know what's funny? I never pegged you to be with a guy like Ricardo," I said laughing and playing around with my dry ass salad.

"I know, but girl, he has straight bank and his dick game is the bomb! So Missy, have you and Paul been hitting it off well?"

"Yeah, he's real cool. We've been talking on the phone and texting each other, but we haven't seen one another. I feel guilty because I'm trying to work things out with Neron," I said.

"Well, you know what I say, ain't anything wrong with having friends," she said laughing and holding her hand up to give her a five. When I didn't laugh at her joke, she looked at me concerned.

BABY MAMA FROM HELL 2

Are you feeling alright?" Renee asked as she grabbed her can and sipped her Mountain Dew.

"Yeah, I can't eat. I'm too nervous about tonight," I replied.

"Nah bitch. You haven't been eating a damn thing during lunch for the past week. You're fuckin' pregnant G," said Renee.

"Damn heffa, can you keep your voice down? I'm not pregnant," I replied.

"Whatever. You're pregnant! I guess you'll be feeling nervous for about nine months," she joked.

It suddenly dawned on me that I could possibly be pregnant. I had missed my period and Paul and I obviously haven't had sex, so I knew Neron was the father. Oh my God! I suddenly felt queasy and began sweating.

"You alright?" Renee asked.

I couldn't respond. I jumped up from my seat and jogged towards the restroom. I burst through the bathroom stall and threw up my Caesar salad. I couldn't stop hurling, so I was throwing up stomach acid and dry heaving. I wiped my mouth with the back of my hand and smiled. I knew fate would bring Neron and I back together. This baby was a blessing.

"Gaby?" Renee called out.

"Yeah," I responded weakly as I opened the bathroom stall and walked out.

"What's wrong?" She asked.

"I fuckin' threw up," I said feeling feeble.

"Yo, I knew it! You're pregnant! I know Neron will be happy about this! Well, what about Paul?"

Damn, I forgot about Paul that quickly.

"I don't want to break the date, so I'll still go out with him tonight. Before I tell Neron anything, I have to make sure I'm indeed pregnant though. I don't want to get his hopes up," I said grinning.

"I'm going to be an auntie," Renee sang as I washed my hands. She hugged me in excitement and we walked out the bathroom together.

*

It was 6 o'clock and I was just getting home. My brother, Jose, had already picked the boys up from their bus stop so, I was able to stop by Walgreens and pick up a pregnancy test. I was so anxious. Paul had my head so far gone that I didn't even realize I had missed my period.

I eagerly tore open the pregnancy test box and peed on the stick. Before I could even wipe myself and flush the toilet, *pregnant* appeared inside the pregnancy test window. My heart jumped for joy. I knew Neron was going to be thrilled about this baby as much as I was. Paul was set to pick me up around seven-thirty tonight, so I needed to be ready. I would figure out how I was going to tell Neron about the pregnancy later.

I swiftly showered, shaved and applied lotion to my body. I sprayed on some of the perfume I had lifted from out of Kimora and Neron's house. I slipped on a simple all black purpose dress. I had straightened my hair bone straight and placed my debit card, drivers' license and my red fire engine lipstick into a knock-off Gucci bag. I popped a mint into my mouth as I put on a pair of silver hoop earrings and a big silver bulky bracelet. I was slipping on some black open toe high-heeled sandals when the doorbell rang.

I grabbed my clutch and walked into the living room to see Jose grilling Paul. I smirked seeing my thirteen-year-old brother trying to be the *man* of the house.

"So, where are you taking my sister," Jose asked with his arms folded and a scowl on his face.

"We're going to dinner," Paul said smiling.

"Where at?" My nine-year-old brother, Diego, asked as he looked from the television.

"The Melting Pot," Paul said looking up and smiling even wider when he seen me.

"What time will you have her home," asked Mario.

Before Paul could respond, I answered for him. "Boys, it's okay. Paul is a gentleman and I will be home soon. Jose, you know the drill. Don't open the door for anyone. There are TV dinners in the freezer and I left ten dollars in case of an emergency. I'm going to need that ten back Jose," I said smiling because I always said the same thing about the emergency money I left for them.

"I know! It's for an emergency only," said Jose rolling his eyes and smirking.

I blew the boys a kiss. Paul told them goodnight as he opened the front door for me, but they didn't respond to him. They were so overprotective of me. I hoped Paul didn't take them being standoffish as being rude.

"Sorry about my brothers," I said as we stepped outside and he closed the front door behind us. The night's air felt amazing as I watched the palm trees sway in the wind. It was windy, but still humid. Even standing so close to Paul had my body temperature rising. Paul placed his arm around my waist as he guided me towards his 2014 black Dodge Durango with tinted windows.

"Nah, they're good. I would be the same way if I had a sister. They're just looking out for you. You can't blame them because you're looking stunning tonight," he said opening the passenger door for me.

"Thank you! You're looking really handsome too," I said grinning as I slid into the car seat.

Paul looked smooth and sexy as he sported some blue Levi jeans with a plaid shirt and some white Van's. He definitely had a different look going on, but it worked really well for him.

The drive to the restaurant was smooth and comfortable. Paul played some Big Sean and turned the volume on low.

"You know I've been thinking about you a lot. Nigga couldn't wait to see your fine ass," he said reaching for my hand and holding it. His touch felt electrifying.

"I've been thinking about you too," I said beaming.

"I'm feeling you. I would love to see where this shit between us goes," he said expressing himself.

No lie, I knew he was really feeling me and there's no doubt that I was feeling him too, but I didn't know how this thing between us would go since I found out that I was pregnant.

I stared out the window bobbing my head to Big Sean's *All Your Fault* featuring Kanye West. This was my shit.

"Oh, word, you like this joint? This is one of my favorite songs off his new CD," Paul said.

"Yeah, the song is sick," I responded.

We pulled into the parking lot of The Melting Pot and Paul cut off the car.

"I want you to enjoy yourself tonight," he said smiling.

"I'm sure I will," I said blushing.

Paul leaned over the console and kissed me. His breath smelled like he had just brushed his teeth with some Colgate, but all I could think about was this pregnancy. I felt wrong kissing him knowing I was knocked up, but his lips felt too good to break away from. After our kiss, he jumped out the car, opened my passenger door for me and held out his hand. I grabbed his hand as he helped me out of his truck.

As we were walking towards the restaurant holding hands, everything felt so right between us. Our vibe was on a thousand and he was the perfect gentleman. I looked up at Paul and smiled as he talked about his favorite dish at The Melting Pot. The man could hold a conversation and there was nothing sexier than a man that could hold his own, in any department. I looked towards the entrance of the restaurant and spotted Neron and Kimora! Damn Neron looked really good. My stomach instantly felt in knots and I started to feel queasy. *Please don't throw up. Please don't throw up!*

I didn't want Neron to see me. I didn't want him to know that I was feeling another man because I was supposed to be loyal to him. I pulled my hand away from Paul and his eyebrow rose.

"What's wrong?" He asked.

"That's my ex right there with my best friend," I said pointing discreetly.

"Don't pay them any mind. We're here to have us a good time," he replied as he grabbed my hand again.

I nodded my head as we strolled passed them since we already had reservations. I saw the look of surprise on Kimora's face, but Neron looked scared. I wasn't going to cause a scene and pull Paul into my mess, but he was in for a rude awakening if he thought I wasn't going to tell Kimora about our sex tape soon.

Right when Paul went to open the door, Kimora blurted out "I should beat your ass bitch! You were dead wrong for the shit you pulled with the police." I stopped dead in my tracks and yanked my hand out of Paul's.

Paul lightly tugged on my arm to try and diffuse the situation, but I was pissed. Here I was trying to take the high road, for once, and miss thing wanted to try me.

"Beat my ass?" I said pointing to myself and laughing smugly. "You should beat Neron's ass because we fucked while you were out of town bitch! Oh, and I'm pregnant too," I said smirking.

Paul looked at me confusingly and I forgot that I was there with him. *I'm such a fuckin' idiot.*

Neron looked like he wanted to slap the shit out of me, but he still remained silent.

"You would say anything to get him back Gabriela, but you're sick bitch! You need to move on. I regret that we were even friends," Kimora shouted as she tried to walk up on me. Neron pulled her back and he still was quiet as a mouse.

"Oh, you ain't told her Neron? Tell her how we fucked the night she was due back in town! Tell her how I made your toes curl as you shot that sweet nut inside me," I shouted, smiling wickedly. Kimora turned to look at Neron and I noticed how his jaw was flinching. He was furious.

"Man, Gabriela you're crazy bruh. I don't even have shit to say to you," Neron finally said.

"Bitch you're delusional. You wished that you could have a sample of my man's dick again. Bitch you jealous," she said sticking her tongue out at me.

"Oh, I'm delusional. Bitch, I have it on camera. Yeah, I sucked him off real good then I rode that dick into town. Yee haw trick!"

"You stupid bitch," yelled Kimora as she thrashed around, trying to break free out of Neron's grasp. I loved seeing her get mad. I now lived to get under her skin.

"Oh yeah, that was my umbrella that I left at your house and I stole your perfume too," I shouted.

I dug into my purse and pulled out my camera memory card. I already made a copy so she could have this one for all I cared. I tossed the memory card towards them.

"There's proof," I said smiling, feeling all giddy inside.

I watched Kimora pick up the memory card and I grinned. Just then, a manager rushed towards us.

"I'm going to have to ask you all to leave. You're disturbing customers and I can't have the chaos on my property," said the manager who looked like he was barely twenty years old.

Paul walked off towards the car as I shot Kimora a bird. To say she looked pissed was an understatement. Neron started to pull Kimora in the opposite direction of the parking lot because she was trying to come for me.

"Neron, I'm indeed pregnant! I took a test today," I shouted!

"Fuck you!" Neron yelled as they walked off with Kimora shouting and cursing.

I turned my attention towards Paul and he was nowhere to be found. I trotted back towards his Dodge Durango and he was sitting inside, smoking a cigarette. I opened the passenger side door and slide inside.

"What the fuck was that Gaby? Man, you're pregnant? I've never been so embarrassed in my life. You causing all this drama and for what! I don't cause scenes Shorty. What if that nigga wanted to get buck, I would've been dragged into your mess and I ain't for all this high school shit," he replied calmly. I could tell he was hurt and was trying to keep his composure.

"I'm really sorry Paul. I just found out today that I'm pregnant. I was going to tell you eventually, but I'm still in shock myself. I still have feelings for that man. I really was going to walk off and ignore them, but as always she had to have the last word. I fucked up our date and I'm sorry," I said sadly.

I truly was upset that I had ruined our first date and dragged Paul into my crazy drama, but I was tired of Kimora thinking she was better than me. I was about to have Neron's baby, again and she was jealous.

"Look, I'm going to take you home. I like you and everything, but this shit ain't cool," said Paul cranking up his truck and putting out his cigarette.

"I understand," I said sighing.

Paul and I didn't talk at all during the drive home and he didn't even bother to put on any music. It was beyond uncomfortable. From texting Paul and talking to him a few times on the phone was helping me keep my mind off of Neron. I didn't want to slide back down and start having Neron withdrawals. I couldn't let things end this way. Hell, things were just getting started between Paul and me.

"Paul, I'm really sorry for what happened, but you knew about all this shit when we first met. I can't change what happened, but maybe we can still make the best of this night," I said looking at him as his jaw tightened.

"Yeah I knew about y'all history, but I didn't know you were expecting. How can we make the best of it? Gaby, I'm really feeling you and I just found out that you're pregnant. I don't know what to think right now," he replied.

"I know it's a lot going on and I'm just as shocked as you are, but I really enjoy your company. Can we please continue the date? Maybe we can go somewhere else."

"Nah baby, I'm taking you home. I appreciate the apology, but this is too much for me," Paul said. I felt terrible.

Paul pulled into my apartment complex and I didn't want to leave him. He walked me to my front door and kissed me on the cheek.

"Have a goodnight," he said walking off.

"Wait! Please give me another chance to redeem myself. I'll even pay for the date," I pleaded. Paul turned around and stood there as if he was weighing the pros and cons.

"Baby, you still love this man and now you're about to have a baby with him. I can't compete with that. I shouldn't have to. It isn't fair to me. I rather us just end this little thing and go our separate ways. I wish you the best though," Paul said.

It felt as if my lips were glued shut because I couldn't say anything. What could I say? I watched Paul turn around and walk off.

Now, here I was pregnant, again and without Neron or Paul. Somebody had to pay.

Chapter 11

Kimora

I couldn't believe what Gabriela just informed me! She fucked my man. My Neron! I was enraged. I wanted to beat the skin off her ass. I wanted to step on this damn memory card, but the woman in me was curious. I had to see for myself because Gabriela had the word liar in her name. I needed to be sure. That bitch kept messing with me. Every time I turned around, her nose was in my relationship, causing problems. Now, here was Neron, quiet as a mouse, trying to weasel his way of out shit. Nah, fuck that!

"Let go of me," I shouted as I snatched my arm out of his grip.

I watched as Gabriela walked away in the opposite direction and I wanted to snatch that bitch up! I stomped off towards his car shouting obscenities.

We were standing at his car and I seriously wanted to do a Tina Campbell on his ass and fuck up his ride. I just couldn't understand why some men couldn't be upfront and honest. That cheating mess wasn't for me. I only had a weakness for one dick and that dick was Neron. I couldn't stay mad or give up on him. I can't explain it, but he got me. He knew that.

"Baby, please let me explain. Man, this shit is crazy," he said, running his hand over his head.

"Explain it, Neron, because I would love to hear you try and talk your way out of this shit," I yelled.

"Baby, please listen to me. She snuck in the night you were due back into town. I was knocked out. She used the key that I keep under the welcome mat for emergencies. The fuckin' lights were out, she smelled like you, and I couldn't see. I thought it was you. I swear I did. I was going to tell you, but I didn't know how because sometimes the best reaction is no reaction. I didn't want to entertain Gabriela. I wanted this whole situation to go away," Neron replied frantically.

"She smelled like me? Boy, is you high?" I replied, pissed off.

"Man, baby, she had on your perfume. You heard her say that she stole it right! I know that smell anywhere. I automatically assumed that it was you. I thought that you might have landed early and came home to surprise me. I had no idea that it was Gabriela's crazy ass. Baby, please. I'm so sorry," Neron begged.

"Fuck you Neron! I allowed you to come back into my life, after you were *engaged* to my best friend. You two had a damn baby together! Now, I'm finding out that after we got back together, ya'll fuck again, but unwillingly to you," I said, sucking my teeth and shaking my head. "And now, she's pregnant again? Then, you didn't even tell me about this shit. Did you know that she recorded this? How am I supposed to deal with that? How am I supposed to trust your ass? Why didn't your punk ass just tell me this shit?" I yelled, running up to him and hitting him in the chest with closed fists.

Neron stood there and took my hits as he kept a straight face. Tears streamed down my face as I realized that we were back to square one in our relationship. Gabriela was about to have his baby, again. She wasn't about to make this pregnancy easy on anyone.

"Mora, baby, I'm so sorry. I wanted to tell you, but I was so scared. The shit sounds like the twilight zone and I was afraid that you wouldn't believe me and leave me. I had no idea that she recorded the shit. Please let me make this right. I thank God every day for having you back into my life. I don't want you to leave me," Neron said as he grabbed both of my wrists and looked me in the eyes.

People were getting out of their cars and stared at him and I as if we were about to duke it out in a wrestling ring.

"For your information, Neron, new pussy ain't better than loyal pussy. You must've forgotten. Do you not see how much drama Gabriela has brought into your life? I might've not liked what you had to say, but I would've respected you if you just came to me and told me what happened. You made me look like a straight fool back there. I know you better not have brought me back anything from that bitch. How do we know if she's even pregnant and if she is, how do we know it's yours?" I ask scrunching up my face and waiting for an answer, but he didn't respond. He just stood there looking at me, ashamed.

"Mora, I'll go get tested. I should've done that first. I'm so sorry. I don't even know if she's pregnant honestly, but if she is, real talk, I'm a possibility because we did mess around. I didn't ask for none of this shit though. You know I wouldn't have intentionally slept with Gabriela. This shit is crazy man." I shook my head at him in disappointment.

"I don't know why we call men dogs because dogs are loyal to their owners. Your ass isn't loyal. Dogs are clean and they obey. I oughta put a collar around your neck with some anti-Gabriela repellant because you just can't seem to stay away from her. You know what? Y'all men are cats. Y'all roam around the streets, y'all sneaky, hardheaded and y'all chase ugly ass rats like Gaby. All I'm waiting for is you to start meowing and I'll be convinced that you're a pussy!" I bellowed.

"Enough Kimora!" Neron shouted.

It took me by surprise to see him get so angry when he was the one who just got caught up.

"I'm sorry this happened. I know the shit sounds crazy, but I didn't know it was Gabriela. I'm telling you the honest to God truth. Let's go home and talk about this some more. We've entertained more than enough people today," he said as he opened up my passenger door.

I slithered my body inside the car and folded my arms across my chest. I didn't know how our relationship was going to survive the mayhem coming our way.

Chapter 12

Neron

I couldn't believe the words that flew out of Gabriela's mouth. This chick was pregnant again. Did I believe it was my baby, I didn't think so. Shit, she was on a date with another nigga, but it was a possibly it could be mine. FUCK! I swear she was ruining my life. I seriously had the baby mama from hell.

We arrived home and Kimora wasted no time jumping out the car and slamming the door shut. Even when she was mad, she was beautiful. I hated causing her pain. I had to fix this and I needed to fix this fast!

I jogged behind Kimora and unlocked the front door. She immediately went towards our bedroom and started to undress. "Baby, we need to finish talking about what happened. I swear I'll do everything in my power to get your trust back. Please don't leave me," I sincerely said.

She ignored me as she threw on a two-piece yellow and blue pajama short set. She grabbed two pillows and walked passed me. "What are you doing?"

"I'm sleeping in the living room until we get a new bed. There's no way that I'm lying in there," she replied as she tossed the two fluffy pillows onto the sofa.

"Do you want to talk about it?" I asked.

She ignored me. She sat on the sofa, scrolling through her phone.

"What in the hell," she mumbled.

"What?" I asked standing over her.

"I'ma beat that bitch ass, Neron. I'm so tired of this shit," she replied.

She passed me her cell phone and one of Kimora's Facebook friends had tagged her in a status in a group called, "Deadbeat Daddies" on Facebook. I read the post and was pissed.

"Neron Lopez is the deadbeat dad of the year! This man will get you pregnant and leave you. He doesn't believe in supporting his kids and is a serial cheater. He uses his current girlfriend Kimora Murphy for money and luxury. She tries to keep him away from his responsibilities as a man and father because she's jealous that I'm now

pregnant with our second kid. Beware of this dog because he has fleas!"

I passed Kimora back her phone and stood up. I paced the floor as I tried to calm down. I was far from a deadbeat and I was never the type of man to mooch off of a chick. My parents paid for my condo as long as I stayed in barber school. I was blessed to be able to focus primarily on school. I had money saved up from jobs I had in high school. I wasn't a big frivolous spender and spent money wisely. I wasn't hurting for shit. Kimora did things for me out of the kindness of her heart. I never asked her to.

"That bitch is always talking shit online. I prefer face-to-face arguments. She knows I don't do that keyboard thuggin'. She must've forgotten that ass whipping I gave her a while back," Kimora shouted.

"Kimora man, you know I'm not using you, baby. I've told you before that the only thing I want from you is your love. Please talk to me. You know her crazy ass is making shit up and you know damn well I'm not a deadbeat. I had Gabriela living with me and was taking care of her ass."

"I hear you. I need to be left alone right now," she said honestly.

I decided to give her some space and let her get her mind right. I didn't want to keep pushing her to talk if she didn't want to so I just grabbed my keys and jetted. I was going to holla at my boy Quan because after a day like this, a few drinks were definitely calling my name.

*

"Bruh, I've never been so fuckin' stressed in my life. Every time Kimora walks out the front door, I'm always scared that she isn't going to come back to a brotha," I vented to my boy Quan.

I was sitting outside Mama Pam's house on the porch, catching Quan up on all the craziness that is called my life lately. I needed to vent because Gabriela was driving me nuts! My boy Quan always had good advice for me, and if he didn't, I'm sure Mama Pam did.

"Damn. Yo, do you think she's really pregnant? I'm sorry bruh, but that chick is loopy as Fruit Loops. She got some issues. I would've Kevin Gate's her ass if she snuck up in my house and *tried* to fuck me. I would've tossed her ass off of me so quick and used my cell phone light to verify her identity whether the pussy was good or not! You know I don't give a damn," said Quan as we shared a laugh. He wanted to be a damn comedian today, but I needed that laugh.

"But, I feel sorry for you though man. I hate you gotta deal with that broad," said Quan turning up his beer and swigging down the contents.

"With Gaby, you never know if she's telling the truth though. I need to meet with her. I need to see if this shit is true or not. I can't tell Kimora about meeting up with her because she would want to tag along and that shit is a recipe for a disaster," I said, cracking open another can of beer.

"I should body slam your ass right here on this damn lawn," said Quan shaking his head.

"Damn. For what?" I asked laughing.

"Leave that chick alone. You don't need any fuckin' proof. That's just going to create more drama and give her hope because that's exactly what she wants out of you. She wants you to come running her way. I understand your square ass wants answers and all that, but wait nine months and just get a DNA test done. Ain't no way I would be investing my time to figure out her story," Quan said matter-of-factly.

"I'on know, man. I need proof. There's no way I can live my life for the next nine months not knowing. I just ain't that type of dude my nigga," I replied.

"Well, go ahead and be stupid. You know I have three baby mamas and I wasn't in a relationship with none of them when they popped up and said that they were pregnant. I ain't give them a dime nor sign that birth certificate until I was ninety-nine percent sure they were my seeds. We got the test done right in the hospital and got the results back ASAP. When my three badasses came back to be my kids, I was there since day one they popped out the coochie. I guess you feeling a type of way because she had your first daughter. Do your thang, but I wouldn't meet up with her if I were you," replied Quan lighting a Black N Mild.

"Hey, boys! Come inside for dinner," yelled Mama Pam.

Quan and I trotted inside the apartment because she could throw down. I was never going to decline one of Mama P's meals.

I sat down at the table with Quan as Mama P fixed our plates. She had whipped up smothered oxtails, macaroni and cheese, collard greens and yellow rice.

"Y'all better get y'all asses up and wash yo damn hands!"

"Sorry mama," I replied smiling and kissing her on the cheek.

"Dang, why you always gotta curse mama," said Quan smirking.

"Because it's my damn house and I pay all the bills. Don't question me wit yo black ass," she replied as she smirked.

Quan and I howled. Mama P definitely had no filter.

As we sat back down at the table, Mama placed our plates in front of us. My mouth watered. Since Kimora and I didn't get to have our dinner at the Melting Pot, I was hungry as hell.

"Looks so good mama," I said before bowing my head and saying grace.

"Thanks, baby," said Mama P.

"So, what's going on? You ain't been by to see me in weeks," said Mama P.

"I know. I'm sorry. Things have been hectic," I replied.

"Yeah, he's going through some Lifetime movie type shit," said Quan stuffing his mouth with macaroni and cheese.

"Watch cha mouth, boy, before I smack the macaroni and cheese out cha mouth!" Mama Pam said giving her son the side eye.

Quan paid her no mind as he laughed at his mother and kept eating his meal. I shook my head and filled Mama P in on what was going on with Gabriela and what she thought I should do.

"Damn. You and Quan sure know how to pick these females. Quan already has three baby mamas that I can't stand," said Pam.

"Damn, how my baby mama's get in this ma," said Quan laughing.

"Anyway, look, I'mma tell you like this, if you feel the need to get proof then so be it, but after you get your proof, stay away from her. Don't fall into any of her traps and if she comes near you, you need to handle her ass. No more Mr. nice guy because you don't want to lose Kimora behind all this. I know you might feel guilty about Mia and that might be the reasoning behind wanting to know. I get that, but after you hear what you're looking for, leave her be for nine months baby. Now that's all I gotta say," said Pam digging into her food.

"Well, you've said enough," said Quan joking.

We all belted n laughter, changed the subject and ate our food. I chopped it up a few more hours with them and left with their advice on my mind.

*

Well damn, I wanted to give Kimora some space, but it had been three days since we saw Gabriela at The Melting Pot. Tension had been so thick around the house with Kimora and me. She never was home and when she was, she barely speaks to me. It was like she was avoiding me. Graduation was this weekend and I was hoping Kimora was coming home to come with me to celebrate and cheer me on.

While Kimora was out running around, I decided to go by Gaby's mother's house. I tossed on a pair of crisp white shorts with a red and black button up shirt. I slipped on a pair of black Air Forces Ones. I made the drive to Gabriela's house quickly and to my surprise, she was home. When she opened the door, she looked like I was Publishers Clearing House presenting her with a check for life or some shit. She was excited as hell to see me. It was creepy.

"Oh my God, Neron, baby what do I owe the pleasure of seeing you today? Come inside," Gabriela asked, smiling. She was wearing a sleeveless black and aqua V-neck Maxi dress. Her hair was tied into a messy ponytail.

"Cut the bullshit, Gabriela! There's no damn way I'm coming inside your shit," I said teed off.

I looked passed her and all eyes were on me. I forgot about the possibility of her brothers being home. All three of her little brothers came outside the front door and greeted me. They were cool and I still had love for them, but if only they knew how crazy their sister was.

"Boys, go back inside please," Gaby asked them.

One by one, they filed into the house, but not before Jose gave me some dap. Gabriela then smiled as she closed the front door behind her and we stood outside.

"What sick game are you playing?" I asked, seething with anger.

"This isn't a game. I love you, Neron. I can't just forget about you. I can't just let you go. I figured if I trapped you, you would love me and treat me how you did when I was pregnant with Mia," she replied, looking like a lost puppy.

"Do you hear yourself? You sound crazy as hell. I've moved on and from what I saw the other day, so have you," I replied.

"I tried to move on, but he isn't you. We only hung out twice and no, nothing happened between us if that's what you're thinking," Gabriela said.

"I don't give a fuck what happened between y'all. You're not my woman and you never will be again."

Gaby immediately started crying. She knew I used to be a sucker for her when she cried because she looked so cute, but those days were over.

"Take this test," I said passing her a pregnancy test box.

"Are you serious," she asked, sniffling.

I twisted up my mouth and gave her an expression that suggested I was indeed serious. She took the hint, sucked her teeth and walked inside the house, leaving the front door open. I guess she thought I was coming in behind her, but she had me messed up if she thought that was going to happen.

I patiently stood outside, waiting for her to return with my back and right foot against the concrete wall. This test could change my life. I never thought I would be back in this predicament with Gabriela. It was fucked up that our daughter had passed away, but I had moved on and now she had slithered her unstable creepy ass back into my life and could possibly be pregnant with my kid, again. Man, this shit was crazy. I blew air out of my lips as I thought of all the drama she had been putting Kimora and me through.

Within two minutes, she was back outside. She passed me the pregnancy test and like she had stated, she was certainly pregnant. I wanted to chop her ass in the throat.

"I have an appointment next week. It's the first one so we would get to hear the heartbeat and find out the due date," she beamed. "Would you like to go with me?"

"Fuck no! That's definitely not going to happen. I just needed to know if you were pregnant. That's it! I want a DNA test once the baby is born. Don't call me, email me, Facebook message me, come by my house, or stalk me. I want nothing to do with you until after this baby is born," I said adamantly, looking her straight in the eyes.

"Fine."

"I mean it Gabriela. I'm not playing. I've had enough of you," I said, raising my voice and quickly calming down since I remembered her brothers were home.

She didn't say another word as she just stared at me. I took that as my queue to leave. She made that way too easy, so I knew she had some shit up her sleeve. I was ready for her ass because I'll be damned if she ruins my life.

*

After I had left Gabriela's house, I went to get tested. I meant it when I said I was going to do everything in my power to get Kimora to trust me again. I was nervous as hell getting my blood taken. I prayed Gabriela didn't give me some shit that couldn't be cured. The nurse assured me that my results would be ready before the weekend and that they would call me if something were wrong.

Once I left the clinic, I decided to call Kimora. Every time I called her, she never answered, but to my amazement, this time she did.

"Hello," she answered, sounding sad and defeated.

"I just wanted to call and see how your day was going. I just left the clinic. I get my results in a few days," I replied.

"That's good. I appreciate you going to do that for me," she said.

"No problem. Well, um, would you like to meet up and maybe go to dinner? Are you still coming to my graduation this weekend," I asked.

"I'm still coming, Neron, but I'm not ready to be out on a date with you right now. You're lucky I'm even attending your graduation," she responded bluntly.

"Okay. I understand. Thank you. Well, I guess I'll see you at home. I love you," I said truthfully.

"Yeah, okay," she countered and hung up.

I sighed. It was going to be hard to have her trust me again, but I'm willing to do whatever it takes.

Chapter 13

Kimora

I just hung up with Neron and was sitting at a red light. I would leave the house every day just to get away from the tension between him and me. I decided I was going to watch what was on the memory card that Gaby tossed at me.

Beep! Beep! I looked in my rearview mirror and sucked my teeth. The light was barely green for one second. I hated when someone blew the horn exactly when the light changed. When people do that, I really want to get out of my car, sit on my hood and feed birds for an hour to piss them off. Instead, I pressed on the gas pedal and drove with no destination.

I pulled into a Wal-Mart parking lot and decided to just sit here and get my thoughts together. I inserted the memory card into my phone and my hands trembled as I pressed *play.* I sat there watching Gaby sneak into our home to suck and fuck my man. I couldn't even finish it. It disgusted me when I heard Neron say my name, thinking it was me. I felt a sense of relief knowing Neron was telling the truth because clearly in the video, he was knocked out cold and had no idea what was going on.

Now, you're probably wondering why I'm fighting so hard for this relationship, but I love him. He's my first and only love. I never stopped loving him, even when we broke up. He's not beating or cheating on me. He comes from a great home and he's good to me. He's responsible and has a good head on his shoulders. He's about to graduate from barber school and has held a goal of opening up his own barbershop since he was a little boy. Not to mention, he's a beast in the bedroom.

I told myself that I was never going to be the type of woman that fought over a man, but if Gaby thought she was going to steal my man and break up our relationship, she had another thing coming. I wasn't going anywhere and if I caught her ass near my man or my house again, I would beat her ass. Pregnant or not!

Immediately I went home and ordered a new bedroom set from off the Internet. If things were going to get back to normal, then the bed had to go. Even though I only needed a new bed, I couldn't resist the cute bedroom set that offered a matching dresser, chest and two end tables that were on sale.

As I finished ordering our new bedroom set, I decided to tidy up the house. After cleaning, I ordered Chinese food. I just wanted to sit home with my man and enjoy his company. I felt bad ignoring him these past few days, but I really needed to get my mind right so I wouldn't say something I didn't mean.

I heard the front door open just as I coming out the shower. I walked into the living room, making sure it wasn't crazy ass running through my house. I smiled when I saw that it was my Neron.

"Hey," he said.

"Hey," I replied slightly smiling.

"Are you alright?" He asked as he hung his keys on the key rack.

"Yeah. I ordered us a new bedroom set and some Chinese. The food should be here in about thirty-five minutes. So, where'd you go?"

"I hung out at Quan's hours for a few hours. You know Mama Pam fed me," he replied patting his stomach.

"Oh, okay. That's cool. Um, I watched the tape," I said staring at him directly in the eyes.

"Why though baby? What did you get outta doing that?" He asked with his face screwed up.

"I just had to see. I'm sorry that I didn't believe you," I said walking up to him.

"It's alright. I would've acted the same, probably even worse if I were in your shoes," he said pulling me towards him and unraveling my coffee colored towel.

My towel fell to the floor and he immediately grabbed my breasts. He lowered his head and licked my nipples as if he was eating an ice-cream cone. He twirled his tongue around my nipple rings and his touch quickly sent chills up and down my body. I watched him swiftly unbuckle his belt, button and unzip his jeans. Neron scooped me up into his arms and pushed my body against the cold wall.

"Shitttt, that's cold," I mumbled.

I wrapped my legs around his waist, interlocked my fingers behind his head and effortlessly, he slid into home base.

"You feel this dick?" He whispered in my ear, not moving, just letting his meat throb inside me.

"Yessssss, I feel it," I replied, panting.

"This is all yours. Ain't another woman on this earth gone ever have it! You hear me," he replied as he pressed his lips against mine.

All I could do was nod my head yes because he had my lips in a tranquil state. He pulled his dick out, slid it back in, pulled out and slid back in again. The shit felt amazing!

He then began to thrust and stroke me like a porn star. It felt so good that I started matching his rhythm and fucked him back as I began to grind on his meat. I grabbed his ass cheeks, pulling him deeper into me.

"Damn, gurl, I love your ass," whispered Neron in my ear as he grunted.

"Fuckkk! I love you tooooooo," I moaned as we enjoyed each other's bodies.

By the time we were done, I was forced to soak my body in a hot bath because I was so sore from the fuck session we had for the last two hours.

*

A few days had passed and things were slowly returning to normal. Since Neron was innocent, after we received our new bedroom set, I moved back into the bedroom. He received his STD and HIV results and everything was normal and negative. It was a huge relief to know that her psycho ass hadn't compromised our health.

*

Neron graduated from Barber school yesterday. I was so proud of Neron. It was nice to see him so happy with everything that had been going on. After the ceremony, his parents presented him with a check for ten thousand dollars as a graduation gift to get his barbershop set up. Combined with the money he had saved from when he was working during high school, he had a nice amount put away in the bank. All he was waiting on was the approval of his bank loan.

Neron's father, a detective who looked identical to the singer Miguel, urged him to get a restraining order. I had accidently mentioned what was going on with Gabriela during his ceremony dinner and his parents were floored. His mother, Lisa, was hysterical. She was always dramatic about anything though. His father, Malik, mentioned how he handles many causes of fatal attraction and Gaby shouldn't be taken lightly, but Neron insisted that he didn't need a restraining order enforced. He said it made him look like a wimp because what man gets a restraining order out on a woman. We didn't argue with him about his decision because, for the most part, Gabriela hadn't contacted us in any form since our restaurant run in. Also, Neron didn't want the possible mother of his second child, to be in jail or on papers. His father assured him though, that if he heard about Gabriela coming out of pocket again, he was going to make sure she was thrown in jail for some serious charges, with or without Neron's consent. Things were finally looking up for us and all we needed was the DNA test to come back showing that he wasn't the father and we could really move on from this.

*

While Neron was out finalizing some things with his shop, I decided to cook him a nice dinner. He's been working so hard and I just wanted to reward him for all his hard work. I was in a great mood since I just got back from being pampered. I had got my eyebrows waxed, a manicure and pedicure. I even stopped by the salon and got the red rinsed out of my natural Tracee Ellis Ross type hair.

I was prancing around the kitchen as I put the food on plates. We were having steak, loaded baked potatoes and peas. On the middle of our dining room table, I had a bottle of champagne chilling in an ice bucket. On the side of the ice bucket were two lit candles and among the rest of the table were scattered pink and red roses. Everything was exactly how I wanted it to be. My lips curled into a smile as I heard the keys jiggling in the front door. I quickly stood in front of the door with a sexy red seamless chemise.

"Damn gurl," said Neron as he entered our apartment.

"I just wanted to do something special for you. Things are looking up for us and I just wanted to show you how much I love you and how hard I ride for us," I said slowly strolling towards him.

Neron dropped the keys on the floor as I pushed him roughly against the wall. Our bodies were pressed together like peanut butter and jelly. I leaned in and kissed his warm and soft lips and they felt like heaven against mine. He grabbed a lock of my hair and held on for dear life as he inserted his tongue into my welcoming mouth. My emotions were like fireworks. Neron grabbed a handful of my ass as we broke our kiss. I looked up into his eyes as they stared back into mine.

"I love you," he said whispering the magical three words that I loved to hear so much.

"I love you more," I said pulling away from him and grabbing his hand. I led him towards our dining room table and he instantly smiled.

"Damn! Everything looks good," Neron said as he pulled out my chair.

"Thanks," I replied.

We bowed our heads and said grace. Neron dug into the food like I knew he would. He loved my cooking.

"Baby, why aren't you eating?" Neron asked.

"Umm, you see the size of the peas?"

"Um, yeahhh! I'm eating them, how can I not?" He replied, grinning and looking confused.

"Well, Um, that's how big your baby is right now," I respond nervously.

Neron dropped his fork and it clanked against the glass plate. He grabbed a linen napkin and wiped his mouth. I had found out I was pregnant a few days ago. I was slightly over six weeks and I was nervous to tell him with everything going on with Kimora.

My heart was thumping as I watched Neron get up and walked towards me. I couldn't read his emotions. He walked over towards me and got on bended knee. He grabbed my hand and that's when I noticed a few tears slipped from his eye. *Oh goodness, he's crying.* The sight of him crying before me melted my heart and made me fall in love with him even more. I didn't even know that was possible. I truly loved this man before me.

"Kimora, baby, you have no idea how happy I am to hear this news. Girl, I love you so much and you're about to give me a baby. Man, this is the happiest moment I've had in a long time," he said kissing the back of my hand and gently pulling me to stand on my feet. He hugged me as he said "thank you" over and over. I started to cry with him. I didn't expect him to take the news so well.

"I thought you would be mad," I mumbled.

"Why would I be?" He asked.

"Because of Gabriela," I responded.

"I know things are crazy right now, but never would I be mad at you carrying my baby. I'm going to be with you for the rest of my life. This is great Mora," said Neron as he lightly grabbed my chin and pecked my lips.

Needless to say, we didn't get to finish dinner because Neron made love to me all night long. It's a good thing I was already pregnant because if I weren't, after tonight, I definitely would've been.

Chapter 14

Neron

My barbershop, The Fade Shop, was set to have its grand opening in a few weeks. I had got approved for a loan and found a location right away. The grand opening was going to be everything because I was going to have a live DJ, giveaways and a few local celebrities like the comedian, Lil Duval stopped through. Things were going to be all the way live.

I had hired six of the sickest barbers Jacksonville had to offer. They were beasts with the clippers. I even had a female barber on my team. Opening up this barbershop was a dream come true. Plus, I needed some money to start coming in since Kimora was now eight in a half months pregnant! We've decided not to find out the sex. It was her wish, so I went along with it. She's due a few weeks apart from Gabriela. I'm not going to lie; it caught me by surprise when she told me that she was pregnant.

It had been hard to even fully enjoy her pregnancy and be happy because I was about to possibly have two newborns at the same damn time. Now, don't get me wrong, I was thrilled about becoming a father again, but I was worried how all of this was going to play out with Gabriela. Speaking of her, I hadn't heard anything from her, surprisingly. She hadn't reached out to me at all and I'd been relieved, not hearing from her.

*

The day finally arrived. It was the grand opening of The Fade Shop out in the St. Johns Town-Center. To see all my ideas come together finally felt amazing. A nigga felt like Jay-Z or some shit!

Kimora was right by my side as I cut the bright red ribbon. Hundreds of folks quickly flocked inside the shop as photographers snapped pictures left and right. I felt like the man. I was giving out free haircuts from 10pm until 2pm today. The DJ was playing some of the latest hits and there were even refreshments for everyone.

I mingled around my shop, talking and interacting with everyone when I spotted Gabriela. *Not Today Satan. Not today!*

I quickly scurried towards Gaby to keep a scene from happening. Kimora must've been somewhere in the back because as I frantically looked around, I couldn't see her. I lightly grabbed Gaby's arm and ushered her outside in a casual manner so people wouldn't be alarmed.

"What are you doing here?" I asked through clenched teeth.

Gabriela stood there holding the small of her back and smiling as if I was supposed to be happy to see her ass. Her stomach looked like it had three babies inside, instead of one. She was carrying it well though because she hadn't gained any weight anywhere else but her stomach. Her nose had spread too, but, for the most part, she looked the same besides having a bigger stomach of course.

"I've let you off the hook for too long. I need some money," she said rubbing her thumb repeatedly across her other four fingers. "These doctor bills aren't cheap and by the looks of your shop, I see you're doing pretty well. So, I need you to cut me a check baby daddyyyy," she sang. She was now rubbing her belly and looking around, I guess trying to spot Kimora.

"Man, I told you that I didn't want anything to do with you until after we have the DNA test. You ain't getting shit from me. You better get on Medicaid or some shit because I ain't giving you a dime," I mumbled. I was really trying to maintain my cool, but this chick was pissing me off.

"I didn't lie down and fuck myself! You helped make this baby," she replied, putting her hands on her hips.

"WHAT! You might as well say you damn near lied down and made this baby by yourself because I was sleeping! You know if I was conscious and in my right mind, that shit would've *never* went down," I said getting agitated being in her presence.

"Whatever," she said waving her hand back and forth, obviously disagreeing with what I was saying. "Look, you haven't even asked me what we were having. Your *daughter* is hungry Neron. I see y'all serving food, let your baby mama get a plate," she said looking around.

Daughter? Wow, I get another chance to have a princess. Hearing Gabriela say that she was having another girl really excited me, but I couldn't get too wound up until I found out if that little girl were mine.

"Gabriela, this is my place of business. I need you to leave," I said snapping out of my thoughts.

"Don't threaten me, Neron, because I will turn this shit out, for real," she countered, raising her voice.

"I'm the mother of your kids and you treat me like shit. You didn't even invite me to your little grand opening. I only found out because I just happened to see people promoting your shit on Facebook," she said getting vibrant.

"Stop it! Stop this shit, right now," I replied as I saw Kimora walk out of the building, maybe searching for me. *Oh Lord, why did Kimora bring her behind outside?*

I saw Gabriela follow my eyes and I knew she had spotted Kimora. *Fuck!*

"What the fuck Neron," Gabriela shouted.

"Calm down," I said through gritted teeth as customers started to stare.

"She's pregnant too! You got her pregnant Neron! So, what, you were planning to dismiss and ignore my baby and ride off into the sunset with this bitch right here?" Gaby asked, pointing in Kimora's direction.

She tried to run up on Kimora, but I grabbed her arm and held her back. Kimora rubbed her belly and stuck her tongue out at Gaby. That only infuriated her more because Gaby was thrashing around like a manic.

"Kimora quit it! Go inside baby, please," I said as I tried to calm down Gabriela.

Kimora ignored my request and stood there as the DJ came over to try and help me calm down Gabriela as people whispered and stared.

"Fuck you Neron! I swear that I'm going to take you for everything you got bitch! This shop will be mine when I'm done with you! Just watch and see!" She shouted as she snatched away from the DJ and me. She shot me the bird as she wobbled out into the parking lot. She got into her car and sped off erratically, almost hitting a parked car. Not even five minutes after Gabriela sped off, my parents had arrived. Gabriela was lucky my father wasn't here to witness her behavior because she definitely would've got arrested.

I wiped the sweat from my forehead as I stared at Kimora and my customers. This was a damn scene from a movie. I definitely had the baby mama from hell.

"Okay, everyone, let's keep the party going. Grab some refreshments. DJ, spin something real quick for us.

This is supposed to be a party y'all," said Kimora clapping her hands and trying to get everyone back into the swing of things. Slowly but surely, folks started to mingle and eventually Gabriela was a distant memory for my customers.

I grabbed Kimora's hand as we smiled and thanked people for coming out as we strolled towards my office. Inside my private office, I sat down at my oak wood desk and put my head into my hands.

"What was that all about Neron?" Kimora asked as she stood by the door, staring me down.

I knew she was mad about all the shit that just popped off, but I was glad my baby girl knew not to make a scene. It was sexy when a woman knew when to wear her ratchet hat, freak hat, and business hat. My baby was a jack-of-all-trades. I was glad she kept her business hat on and didn't get ratchet at my grand opening and try and get at Gaby. I blew air out of my lips though because I knew it wouldn't take her long to ask what Gaby was doing here.

"She just showed up. She was asking for money and freaked out when she saw that you were pregnant. It set her off," I said, inhaling and exhaling.

"If this baby turns out to be yours then you need to petition for full custody because we cannot be tied to her for life Neron. We will never be fully happy if she turns out to be the mother of this kid," Kimora said.

I prayed to God that I wasn't the father of the baby she was carrying. I knew I was a possibility, but I hoped like hell I wasn't the baby daddy. I pulled a bottle of Amsterdam peach from out of my desk and poured me a drink. I needed to settle my nerves before I went back out there and mingle with my guests.

Chapter 15

Gabriela

"I can't believe that motherfucker got Kimora pregnant and from the looks of her, we're due weeks, maybe days apart. I wanted to be the only one to have his kids. Why was Kimora always trying to compete with me? I hated the way I showed my ass at Neron's grand opening because he was my man and I'm supposed to ride for him. I need to apologize to him. I just wanted him to acknowledge me. I bet you that he stays rubbing her feet, massaging her back and catering to her while I'm stuck single, lonely, caring for my brothers and depressed. It isn't fair," I said venting to Renee on the phone while I lied on my left side, across my bed.

"Shit. Fuck him! You sound crazy as hell. Y'all aren't together. You did the right thing by showing your ass. I would pop up on his ass every chance I get if I were pregnant with his baby. He needs to run you your money and quit playing. Fuck him! Terrorize his ass every day, but you need to find a new dick and hope off his. Don't go apologizing to him! His ass is straight disrespectful and I hate how you allow him to treat you," Renee yelled coughing in between her words.

"Shit, I need to be over there smoking one with chu right now. My mind is everywhere because I feel everything you're saying, but I still love him," I said trying to get comfortable on the bed.

"Shit, I know plenty of women that smoked weed during their pregnancies. You should come over and smoke one with cha girl so you can forget about all your problems," said Renee.

"Well, I don't want to take the chance of anything happening to this baby, so I can't. I will come chill with chu though, so let me get my ass up and get dressed," I replied as we hung up.

I tossed my phone next to me on the bed as I sat up. It was getting harder and harder to do normal every day activities. I was so over this pregnancy. As I was struggling to find the motivation to get up and get dressed to go to Renee's, the ringing of my cell phone halted my plans.

"Hello," I said.

BABY MAMA FROM HELL 2

"Gabriela?" I knew that voice from anywhere. My heart right away skipped a beat.

"Speaking," I replied while still playing dumb.

"It's Paul. How you been?"

"Oh, hey," I said dryly. "I'm Fine," I lied but felt excited on the inside to hear his voice. My heart fluttered at every word he spoke.

I hadn't talked to Paul in months. I tried texting him and calling him a few times after the restaurant incident, but he never answered or returned any of my text messages.

"You were just on my mind. I heard about what went down with ole boy. I just wanted to see how you were holding up," he said.

I felt like a can of biscuits that was just popped open because I immediately broke down. I couldn't hold the tears in anymore.

"Damn, what's wrong?" Paul asked.

"Everything! Everything is wrong. Nothing is going right. I'm due any day now and have no support or help," I shrieked.

"I'm on my way to your house. Is your address still the same?"

"Yesssss," I said through tears and snot.

Paul said he would be at my house within fifteen minutes. I got off the bed, wobbled to the bathroom, and preceded to clean myself up. I grabbed a hair tie, put my hair in a ponytail, and then brushed my teeth. I texted Renee letting her know that something came up and I would text her later. As I slipped on my house slippers, my door bell rang.

I shuffled to the living room and looked out the front door peephole. Paul stood behind the door, looking so handsome. I opened the door and smiled. You could tell I had been crying because my eyes were bloodshot red and swollen. I stepped aside and allowed him to enter.

"I brought you some ice-cream. I know it's your favorite," he said.

"Thank you! That's the most thoughtful gesture anyone has done for me in a while," I said grabbing the pint size rocky road ice cream.

"Make yourself comfortable," I said walking into the kitchen to get a spoon.

I came back into the living room and sat next to Paul. He grabbed the spoon from out of my hand, scooped up a nice amount of ice cream, and fed me. It felt nice to have some attention. We talked for hours.

"What do you like to do?" He asked.

He was sitting so close to me that I was getting horny and wanted to blurt out, "fucking," but I kept it cute and put that answer on mute.

"I like to draw," I said shyly. Nobody knew about my passion for drawing except Kimora, but fuck that bitch. She didn't count.

"Word? You can draw? Damn, that's sexy," he said licking his lips.

"You think so? I always felt nerdy," I replied, eating more ice cream from my spoon. I was licking the creamy ice cream slowly to entice him. I knew it was working.

"Umm, yeah," he said clearing his voice. "Nah that's not nerdy at all. You got talent. Use it," he replied staring at me and watching me eat my ice cream.

He was so intrigued on how I felt, what my goals were and how I was doing, that those old feelings I had for him started to come back. We definitely picked up where we left off.

After Paul had left, I decided that I was going to drop by Renee's house because sitting in the house, pregnant with so many emotions isn't what's up. The boys were spending the night at a friend's house, so it definitely would be nice to see my girl.

Chapter 16

Kimora

It's been about a week since Gabriela showed her ass at my man's grand opening. I was getting real tired of her. I felt like Neron wasn't putting her in her place. I didn't know if it was because she lost their first child, so he was trying not to stress her out, but I was pregnant too. I hadn't really expressed how I felt to Neron, but I think he was picking up on it because after I had taken my shower, I noticed he had a gift for me on the bed. I wobbled towards our bed and opened up the bag. Inside, there was a beautiful yellow chiffon maternity dress and a pair of three-inch pink, open toe, ankle strap heels. Instantly my lips curled into a smile. He was so thoughtful.

"Neron," I shouted.

"Yeah baby," he said walking into our bedroom.

"Oh babe, I love it! Thank you," I replied as I held up the dress and shoes, admiring everything.

"You know you don't have to thank me. I know things have been difficult since we've got back together, but I just wanted to tell you thank you for rocking with me.

The shop is doing well and soon our baby will be here. Everything is falling into place baby and I love you so much. I want you to enjoy your day," said Neron smiling. He walked up to me and kissed me with such intensity.

"You trying to get some booty before the shower, stop it!" I said playfully as I lightly shoved him away. Neron laughed as he sat down on the bed and watched me get dressed.

"So, how are you feeling about your parents seeing each other, after all these years? Not to mention, your stepmother Adrienne will be there too," said Neron.

"I'm anxious to see everyone, so I hope everyone is on their best behavior. I can't wait to see Quan and Mama P too," I said, attempting to put on my heels but was struggling.

Neron noticed, got on bended knee, slipped on my heels and buckled them for me. He was the sweetest and most thoughtful man, ever. The pregnancy has definitely brought out his sensitive side. I guess he's really nervous about me doing anything on my own because of what happened to Mia. He stood up and held out his hand. I placed my hand into his and he slowly pulled me up from the bed.

"You look beautiful baby. Your skin is so radiant and glowing. You're the most beautiful pregnant woman I've ever seen," he said sincerely. I blushed.

"Thank you handsome, you don't look too bad yourself," I replied while I eyed Neron from head to toe.

You could tell the barbershop was making some coins only after a week of opening because Neron was wearing a red, white and black striped Polo shirt with a pair of black Levi denim jeans, with some white, grey and black Polo shoes. My baby was dressed to impress.

After we had done the once over in the mirror, we left to attend our co-ed baby shower. I couldn't wait to see everyone, but I hoped everyone was going to get along. My mother and I were still working on our relationship, so I was really excited to see her.

*

Neron and I pulled up to a gated community center out at the beach. It was a beautiful day and the sun was shining bright and not a cloud in sight. I wasn't allowed to help with any planning so I couldn't wait to see how everything looked.

The only thing I knew was that, my father and Neron's parents paid for everything. My stepmother Adrienne and Neron's mother, Lisa, helped plan and put everything together. My mother wasn't good at throwing parties and helping decorate, so she opted not to help plan the shower, but she was happy to even get invited. Mama Pam was in charge of food and refreshments, so I was dying to taste some of her cooking.

Neron parked the car and jumped out, quickly helping me out of the car. As we approached the front community door, I was damn near out of breath. Neron held the door open for me and we walked inside the building. Everyone stood up, clapped and shouted. The love was amazing! Tears swiftly welled up in my eyes as I saw everyone.

The place looked amazing! Since I didn't want to know the sex of the baby, the theme was, "Bun in the Oven." There were about twenty assigned tables seated for four placed strategically throughout the room. Placed in the center of each table were baskets filled with four hot buns with a frame next to it that read, "Bun in the Oven Bakery."

It was the cutest thing. Mama Pam did the damn thing with my cake. It was awesome. It was a yummy six layers, cinnamon *bun* cake. Placed on the back of each chair was a cute russet sign that read, "She's got a bun in the oven!" My family and friends certainly outdid themselves on the decorations. I was truly grateful.

My father, Dewayne, Adrienne and Kennard rushed over towards me and hugged me. They looked really good.

"How's daddy's baby girl feeling," asked my father as he hugged me.

"I'm doing good daddy! I'm just ready to drop this load," I said smiling at my brother Kennard. He looked tall as me. *Dang, he's growing fast.*

"Oh my goodness, the baby kicked," shrieked Adrienne, who looked stunning as ever as she rubbed my belly. I smiled at her and we embraced.

"Hey, sis! Do you know what you're having yet?" Kennard asked. He had facial hair everywhere. My little brother was definitely growing up.

"Nope, I told you guys I didn't want to know," I said playfully.

"Where's mom?" I said looking around for her face.

"I don't know baby doll. I guess she hasn't made it yet," said my Daddy.

Neron noticed my expression and quickly grabbed my hand. I hurriedly replaced my frown with a smile as his parents approached us. His mother, Lisa, was beautiful. She looked just like Vivica A Fox and had the personality to match. Neron's father, Angel, was Dominican so every time he saw me, he would literally speak half-English and Spanish sentences to me. He was hilarious!

"Oh boy! Look at that *gran barriga*! I know that's a *chico* in there! It has to be because our Lopez genes are *fuerte*," said Neron's father.

I smiled at his father as we hugged. He was so energetic to be a police detective. He was a comedian like George Lopez.

After I greeted everyone and mingled for a while, the festivities began. I had a blast! We were playing a game of "Applesauce Never Tasted So Good," where a certain amount of guests volunteered to be paired into teams of two. Out of the pair of two, one of the guests puts a trash bags over their clothes and blindfolds themselves. The person blindfolded must try and feed the applesauce to their partner. Whoever finishes their applesauce the fastest is the winner. It was hilarious seeing Quan, Neron blindfolded, and trying to feed their partner. I died laughing because Neron had applesauce all over Mama Pam's face!

"Boy, what in the hell," Mama Pam shouted as she laughed.

My hands were on my knees, as I laughed so hard at the scene in front of me. I looked up and saw my mother walk into the building and behind her was Gabriela!

Chapter 17

Gabriela

After Paul had left my house, I couldn't wait to go by Renee's because I needed to talk. Paul had my head gone and I was definitely feeling him. I needed to tell her about these feelings for him resurfacing because I felt guilty since I was in love with Neron.

I threw on a cute shirt that Renee purchased for me the other day. The shirt read, "Awww…and to think I almost swallowed you." *Renee is a trip. That's my bitch though.* I pulled up a pair of coochie cutter denim jean shorts over my ass. *Yeah, I was pregnant, but I was still fine and didn't give a damn who judged me.* I slipped on a pair of gold flat gladiator sandals and put my long hair into a neat bun.

I penguin walked towards my car and slowly eased my body into the driver seat. I cranked the car and was annoyed when I saw my gas light on. I hated stopping for gas. I hated pumping gas. I hated the smell of gas. The pregnancy made it impossible for me to pump my own gas because I threw up every single time I smelled it. I sucked my teeth as I backed out of my parking spot and headed to the nearest gas station.

Pulling up to pump number five at Gates gas station, imagine my surprise when I spotted Roxy parked in front of me! I swiftly cut off my car and eased my body out of the car. Roxy was pumping her gas and looking at the watch on her wrist as if she was running late. She looked cute. She was thin and her hair was styled in a cute Nia Long short cut. She had on some red denim jeans, a plain black short-sleeved shirt, and a pair of black flats.

"Shit," I yelled as I purposely dropped my keys, trying to get Roxy's attention.

"Gabriela? Wow, you look like you're about to pop, but you're so cute," Roxy said as she walked in my direction. She smiled, and then bent over to retrieve my car keys.

"Oh, hey Miss Roxy! Thank you. How are you?" I asked as she handed me my keys.

"I'm great baby. I'm cancer free and I'm doing well. Kimora and I are still estranged. We're working on repairing our relationship, but she won't let me in her life easily and I deserve it for the way I treated her and

Kennard. Well, I know she's told you all this, so I don't know why I'm rambling."

What in the hell is she talking about? Oh my goodness, she doesn't know that Kimora and I aren't cool anymore!

"I'm just trying to regain her trust and rebuild our mother and daughter relationship. Well, anyway, I'm actually on my way to Kimora's baby shower. Aren't you coming?" she asked widely smiling.

"Um, I'm actually on my way. I just need to get some gas and I guess I'll just follow you," I said grinning.

"I'll pay and pump the gas baby, go back in your car," said Roxy.

"Oh thank you so much," I said smiling.

I was definitely winning! I didn't have to smell nor pump my gas and I was about to crash Kimora's baby shower.

*

We pulled up to the community center and the parking lot was packed. Before I took my maternity leave, my job threw me a mini baby shower. I still had some of the bags in the backseat of my car. I stepped out of my car and my eyes met with Roxy's. I gave her a fake smile. I could tell she was genuinely happy to be here, but I had my own plans for attending this stupid shower. I looked in my backseat and grabbed the bag that had two packs of newborn diapers inside. I glanced at Roxy and she was coming my way with three big bags in her hand and struggling to carry a baby swing box. I offered to carry the bags for her, but she insisted that she could manage. I think it was because her and Kimora still had an estranged relationship and she just wanted to be seen coming *late* to the shower with a shitload of presents.

We walked inside the building as I spotted Neron playing a baby shower game. My God, the man looked amazing and so sexy. My heart felt like it was on steroids because the love I have for Neron was so strong. I spotted Kimora's stupid ass and the sight of her left a bad taste in my mouth. She was howling in laughter. When she finally looked up in our direction, she flipped!

"What in the hell! Mama, what is *she* doing here?" Kimora shouted with her hands on her hips. All of the guests turned and stared at us. I heard whispers and received stares, but I kept a smile on my face as Roxy and I placed our gifts on the gift table. I spotted Neron, taking off his blindfold. He looked shocked to see me. I waved and smiled at him.

"Baby, we saw each other at the gas station and decided to follow each other here. What's the problem?" Roxy asked.

"The problem is this *trick* and I aren't friends anymore mama. She's fuckin' crazy and slept with Neron to trap him," Kimora shouted with a scowl on her face.

Roxy turned and looked at me in shock. "Gaby? Is this true?" Roxy asked me as Neron approached me.

"We're in love Roxy! He's just using Kimora for her money. We're still fuckin' too! He's just stringing you along Kimora," I yelled.

"You're a lie! Get the hell out of here, NOW!" Roared Neron as his father approached us.

"I just wanted to drop off my gift and send my congratulations. I come in peace," I said smirking.

"You used me to get here?" Roxy asked, shockingly.

I ignored her ass when I saw Neron walking towards me. I rubbed my stomach to remind him that I was pregnant because, at that moment, I didn't know what he was going to do. I held my breath with each step he took. When he finally approached me, he roughly grabbed my right arm.

"Listen, here you sick bitch, stay away from us," he bellowed as his father tried to pry his grip from off my arm.

"Let her go, now son!" Neron's father said.

Neron ignored his father and still had a death grip on my ass. His clasp was starting to hurt me. I took my free arm and slapped the shit out of him. It actually surprised him because he released his hand from around my arm and looked like he wanted to retaliate.

"Oh hell no you rice and bean eating whore," shouted Mama Pam as she tried to run towards me. I was grateful that Quan held her back.

"Let me go, Quan! Neron is like another son to me. Ain't nobody gonna put their hands on him while I'm around," yelled Mama Pam as she squirmed around, trying to free herself from Quan's hold around her waist.

Neron's mother Lisa grabbed a knife that was going to be used to cut the baby shower cake. A partygoer stepped in and was able to grab the knife from her.

"I'ma fuck this bitch up," said Kimora, bringing my attention back to her.

Before I could blink, Kimora charged at me, big belly and all. She punched me in the eyes so hard that I fell. I grabbed my stomach; my instincts kicked in. I needed to protect my baby. Flashbacks of my mom beating my ass while I was pregnant with Mia surfaced in my mind. I was dazed. I can't believe this bitch snuck up on me!

"That's what your ass get," barked Mama Pam. "You lucky it wasn't me because I would've stomped the evil outta your ass." Quan tried to muffle his laughter.

I'll let Mama Pam slide because my beef wasn't with her old ass.

"Stop it," Roxy screamed.

I stood up and ran as fast as my belly would allow me and shoved Kimora. She stumbled and fell back on the table, crushing her baby shower cake and ruining her dress. I smirked to myself and thought I was ruining her day.

Neron and her father, Dewayne went and helped Kimora up as she screamed and called me every name in the book. She was trying her hardest to come at me, but they wouldn't let her go.

"You need to leave, or you'll be arrested for trespassing. I think that hit to the eye is punishment enough. You're lucky a punch to the face is all you got," Neron's father said angrily.

Roxy stared at me in utter disbelief.

"I can't believe you, Gabriela. You were supposed to be Kimora's friend and you betrayed her," said Roxy looking sad at what was taken place.

"Mannnnn chu got some nerve. You were hardly around for her either. You betrayed her and Kennard by running the streets and entertaining men. Bitch please!" I shot back.

My comment rubbed Roxy the wrong way. She ran towards me, but Kennard and Dewayne stepped in and tried to defuse the ticking time bomb that threatened to go off.

"You're wrong Gaby! You're wrong for throwing that shit in my face! This isn't about me right now. It's about you! I love my kids. I wasn't the best mother, but I'm here now to make things right," Roxy defended through her tears.

"Oh please! Save your tears. Somebody, please bring out some violins," I spat tossing my hands up in the air. Roxy was stunned to hear me talk that way to her.

"Don't look surprised! I was the one picking up the pieces after you left Kimora alone to take care of Kennard for days. I was there when she had her first period. I was there when she needed a shoulder to cry on. Not you!" I screeched.

"Somebody get this fake ass J-Lo out of here before I drag her ass," Mama Pam bellowed. Quan held onto Pam for dear life as she tried to free herself. I wasn't worried about her though. My issue wasn't with her.

"You're grimy as fuck Gaby! I swear if I weren't pregnant I would give you the ass whooping of a lifetime," Kimora roared.

"Fuck you Kimora! Bitch I'ma see you once I drop this load too and I'mma fuck you up," I yelled.

"Fuck you! I'ma catch you trick and I'ma be all over yo ass like Velcro. I still have Neron and will always be here. Find your baby daddy hoe," Kimora shouted.

Her words went in one ear and out the other. I trotted out of the community center, leaving behind a room full of stunned people. I accomplished what I came for, to ruin Kimora's shower.

*

I was so pissed off at how Kimora snuck me. My eye was beginning to swell. I needed to talk to Renee. I felt my blood boiling and my nerves were shot through the roof. Too bad I can't smoke or have me a damn drink. Kimora was going to have another thing coming if she thought she was just going to hit me and get away with it.

I drove to Renee's house like a bat out of hell. I was surprised that I didn't get a speeding ticket. I pulled into her complex parking lot and cut off the car. I pulled down my sun visor and inspected my eye again. It was red and puffy. I sucked my teeth and eased my body out of the car.

I wobbled towards Renee's front door and knocked. No answer. I knocked again, still no answer. I became worried. I decided to see if the door was unlocked. I grabbed the knob and twisted it and the door opened. I entered her apartment and saw a man walking butt naked, dick swinging towards her bathroom!

"Um, where's Renee," I asked.

At that moment, Renee came out of her bedroom with an ocean blue sheet wrapped around her body.

"He's about to leave now Gaby. Just chill on the sofa and I'll be out in a minute," she said proudly. There was never any shame in Renee's game.

I shook my head and sat down. After five minutes, the mystery man walked passed me and out the front door. Renee walked into the living room with basic cotton shorts on and a white tank top on.

"Um, I don't think so heffa! You got sex sweat on you," I joked as she attempted to hug me.

Renee disregarded what I said and hugged me anyway. "Girl, what happened to your eye?" She shouted.

"I was on my way over here sooner, but I ran into Roxy, Kimora's mother at the gas station. She just got out of a coma, but before that happened, she and Kimora haven't had the best relationship and they're trying to repair it. Anyway, she had no idea that Kimora and I weren't friends anymore," I said running out of breath from talking so fast. Renee sat there glued to my mouth, so I quickly continued.

"Well, Roxy asked if I was attending the baby shower and I said yes and would follow her to the location. Long story short, I crashed Kimora's baby shower! She punched me and I was only able to push her but she fell on her cake, ruining her dress," I said cackling.

"Gurlllll," Renee dragged out. "You're crazy! Bitch you're the baby mama from hell," she said laughing. I didn't find that funny.

"Not funny! I love that man," I replied.

"But he doesn't love you, hun. You need to let him go and just focus on co-parenting with him," she said.

"Nah," I quickly said, dismissing her idea.

Renee and I sat around talking while she smoked. I stuffed my face with some leftover spaghetti she had in the fridge. I was tearing that shit up!

"Fuck, I gotta pee," I said as I cleaned the last bit of noodles and sauce off my plate. "I'm so tired of going back and forth to the bathroom," I said.

"Better you than me," Renee said grinning like a fool, high as hell. I playfully rolled my eyes as I stood up. I was barely able to take two steps when my water broke!

"Oh my God," I shouted as I looked down and saw the puddle around me.

I turned and looked at Renee as she rushed towards me.

"I don't have my hospital bag with me," I uttered.

"We will figure that out. Let's just get you to the hospital safely," Renee said as she grabbed our purses, cell phone, her blunt and her keys.

"Why do you need that?" I asked referring to her blunt.

"I've never experienced anything like this in my life! I need it," she said looking crazy. She was acting like she was the father of this baby because she was trying to keep me calm, but I could see she was nervous.

The contractions began and boy were they strong. I silently prayed that my unborn daughter would be delivered healthy and safe. I hoped I wouldn't have a repeat of baby Mia. I needed Neron!

"Ooooooh," I said breathing through a contraction.

"Do that he who shit pregnant women do," said Renee trying to be of comfort.

"That crap doesn't work! Oooooh! Neronnnnnn, call my baby daddy," I replied in pain.

"We will do all that when we get to the hospital. Let's go," said Renee guiding me out the door as I held my belly.

Chapter 18

Neron

That bitch! I thought to myself. I hated calling a woman out of their name, but damn Gabriela was the exception. I wanted to beat Gabriela to knock some sense into her ass. That girl tested all my patience. She got on my nerves, in my nerves and around my nerves. I'd been keeping my distance from her yet she still slithers her way into my life. I watched Kimora go off about what just happened as her mother and my mother took her to get cleaned up. I felt terrible that her special day was ruined. The guests sat looking like deer's caught in headlights.

"Mama, tell some jokes or something," I heard Quan tell Mama Pam.

"Boy shut up! I don't know any damn jokes," Mama P shot back.

"I can't tell! The way you roasted Gaby says otherwise," Quan replied laughing.

Mama Pam cracked a smile and rolled her eyes.

"Okay y'all, um, the damn cake is ruined, but we have other refreshments that I've made, so help yourselves," said Mama Pam.

While Mama P contained the other guests, I stepped outside to get a smoke. This chick was like a mosquito during the summertime, just bugging me. I heard the front door open as Quan stepped outside.

"Yo man, that shit was wild. You alright, brah?" Quan asked as he lit a Black N Mild.

"Hell nah!" I said, trying to stay calm.

"Shit I have three baby mamas, but you seem to have more drama than me man," replied Quan.

Just as Quan finished his sentence, my cell phone rang. I didn't know the number and it wasn't blocked, so I answered the call and put it on speakerphone.

"Yo," I said into the receiver.

"Hi, this is Renee, Gaby's friend," said the caller.

"Man, tell that bitch to leave me alone! I don't want shit to do with her until the baby is born," I roared.

"She's in labor! We're at the hospital. I was just calling to inform you."

"How did you get this number?" I asked.

Quan scrunched up his forehead at what he was hearing.

"Gabriela gave it to me," she replied.

"I told that crazy girl to contact me once the baby is *born!* Not when she's in labor."

I need to change my number. How in the fuck did she get my number when I first blocked her from calling and then got a new number?

"Look, I'm just trying to be there for my friend. She's having your baby. You need to be here," said the woman.

"Mannnnn, I ain't trying to hear none of that. I'm a possibility. I don't know if that's my baby. The girl is fuckin' crazy," I said hanging up on her and blocking her number.

It's like Gabriela knew when I was doing well in my life because she always tried to stop my shine and block my happiness. She was like Scar from the Lion King. She was a hater. Since I didn't love her ass, she wouldn't let me be happy and move on. Something had to give.

I walked back into the building and the guests were now eating and chatting. I walked into another room of the building and saw Kimora looking delicious. My baby knew she was bad.

My mother went out and purchased Kimora another dress and a pair of shoes to match. The dress was a mint green spaghetti strap dress that stopped just above the knees. On her feet were mushroom colored closed toe heels.

"You look beautiful baby," I said admiring her.

She didn't respond. I know she was pissed at what just went down, but I had nothing to do with Gaby showing up. Her mama did.

"Oh, so, you're not talking to me?" I asked, standing in front of her.

"Neron, please get out my face," she replied, attempting to walk past me.

"How are you mad at me? Ms. Roxy invited her," I said.

Roxy gasped and put her hand on her chest dramatically.

Kimora stopped in her tracks and turned to look at Roxy.

"Mama, why did you bring her here?" She asked her mother.

"Baby, I had no idea that y'all weren't cool anymore. You and I have been trying to work on our relationship and you barely let me into your life. You never mentioned anything about Gabriela. I had no idea that she was even pregnant. I wouldn't have invited her if I knew you two were through. You have to know that," said Roxy.

Kimora stood there staring at her mom as Roxy stared back with pleading eyes.

"It's okay mom. You're right. I'm sorry," she said exhaling. "Let's just focus on salvaging this baby shower. I'll handle Gabriela later," Kimora said as she walked to her mom and hugged her.

My mother, Roxy, Kimora and myself trotted back into the main room of the building and continued the shower. They had a nigga playing all types of baby games. Let me tell you, I was the master at guessing what type of chocolate was smashed into the baby diapers.

We ended up having a good time though. We received everything. We seriously don't have to come out of pocket for anything. We received a crib that has a changing table attached to it. As the baby grows, the crib converts to a toddler bed. We received the greatest invention ever, a diaper genie. We were given boxes of diapers, diaper rash crème, bottles, bibs, clothes, rattles, blankets, baby lotion, an electric breast pump, baby swing, bassinet, baby shampoo, baby powder, and baby gas drops. You name it, we got it!

I noticed Quan had disappeared with some of my boys for quite some time. I was about to call Quan crazy ass when I saw my boys walk into the room with a big box.

"Attention!" Quan said looking around the room.

I was nervous as hell to see what this fool was about to say.

"Now our boy is about to step into fatherhood and we've enjoyed this baby shower and everything, but all the attention is on lovely Kimora and then the attention will be obviously, towards the baby. Fathers are last," said Quan grinning.

"Sooooo, we, your boys," said Quan pointing to my other friends. "We got cha back! We prepared this lovely man-shower basket for you," said Quan talking in a feminine voice.

Everyone was cracking up as Quan walked towards me with a brown UPS looking box. I was afraid to open the damn thing knowing Quan and my boys, Charter, and Howard.

I opened the box to find a black Dude Diaper Bag. Inside the bag was two types of brown liquor, Hennessy, and Captain Morgan Black. Also, there was a gag gift called daddy's diaper changing tool belt. The tool belt held everything you needed to change a diaper such as wipes, goggles, diaper rash crème, baby powder, and gloves. The shit was hilarious to see the gloves and goggles. There were also three cigars inside. My boys went all out.

"Aw, man, thanks y'all," I said laughing.

Kimora was laughing so hard at the goggles and gloves to change a baby diaper. It was nice to see the shower turnaround from drama to having a good time.

I gave my boys dap and thanked them again as the shower came to a close. Kimora and I began thanking everyone and took pictures with our guests as everyone was quickly exiting the building.

I glanced over and saw Dewayne and Roxy chatting. For the entire duration of the shower, they barely said two words to one another. I walked near them to ease drop. I slowly took my time, picking up paper plates and clearing the tables near them.

"I didn't appreciate you taking my kids from me Dewayne. I wasn't an unfit mother," said Roxy crossing her arms across her chest.

"They needed a stable environment and I gave them that Roxy. You weren't around. Kimora is grown and Kennard is just about. Let's just let bygones be bygones and move on," replied Dewayne, stuffing some meatballs into his mouth.

Roxy shook her head and I saw her getting emotional.

"You're right. I regret it every day. I wish I were around more. After the divorce, my freedom went to my head. I really want to make things right with my kids," said Roxy defending herself.

"Well, make it right," said Dewayne as Kennard approached them.

My ass was mingling with them, getting every single detail. I saw Kimora eyeing me as she poured herself some punch. She shook her head and laughed. I knew she wanted the damn tea just as much as me.

I watched the three of them talk and interact and Kennard seemed like he was genuinely open to having her in his life again. He was just smiling as Roxy talked about how tall he was getting. I noticed Adrienne gave them their space and she kept her distance. Roxy and her only introduced themselves and said nothing more. I guess Roxy wasn't feeling her being the stepmom to her son, but hey, it is what it is.

Once everyone all the guests left, it was just our parents, Pam and Quan sticking around. I wrapped my arms around Kimora, who was standing next to the refreshment table, sipping more damn juice. The girl was punch wasted!

I love you gurl," I said to Kimora.

"I love you too baby," she replied with a forced smile.

"What's wrong?" I asked.

"I'm starting to have contractions. They've been happening for about the last two hours. They're getting pretty intense," she said with pain etched on her face as she placed her cup down on the table.

"Oh my Lord, why haven't you said something?" I asked a little too loudly.

"I wanted to enjoy my shower since it started off rough. I didn't want to worry anyone and they weren't five minutes apart, but now they are! Ooooooooowwwwww," Kimora said as she doubled over in pain.

My parents, Kimora's parents, her brother, Quan and Mama Pam rushed over.

"She's in labor!" I said panicking.

"OH MY GOD! WHERE'S THE HOSPITAL BAG?" I shouted, freaking out.

"Calm down baby. You need to relax so she will stay calm," said my mother.

"It's…it's in the trunk. Remember you packed it the day I found out I was pregnant?" Kimora said through deep breaths

"Okay, that's good. Let's go," I said, walking towards the exit.

"You're forgetting your woman, Neron!" Mama Pam yelled.

Damn! I'm nervous as hell. How in the world was I going to forget my girl?

I turned around, took a deep breath and rushed back towards Kimora to help her to the car. My mind was scrambled like eggs. I was a wreck!

I hated seeing Kimora in pain, but I was so excited to get ready to meet my baby.

Chapter 19

Gabriela

"What did he say?" I said, breathing through contractions.

We had made it to the hospital and I was quickly admitted. I was four centimeters. The doctor wouldn't administer an epidural yet. He wanted me to wait but fuck him! I was the one in excruciating pain! The pain was unbearable, but somehow, someway, all I could think about was Neron.

"He hung up on me! He said to call him once the baby is born and not while you're in labor," said Renee looking sad.

"Are you serious?" I shrieked in disbelief.

"Yeah, I'm sorry girl. He said you're crazy and all this bull shit. Fuck him! We need to focus on you. We need you to deliver a healthy baby girl. You can deal with him later," she said sitting on a sofa near the hospital bed.

"I'm going to kill him," I shouted as a contraction shot through my body.

I know I didn't mean that, but shit these contractions were worse than period cramps.

Renee stood up and jogged towards me. She grabbed my hand and I squeezed the life out it.

"Dammmmmm," shouted Renee.

"I need drugs," I cried out.

Renee trotted out of the room to get the doctor. When she left, the monitor that was observing the babies heart rate started to beep rapidly. I instantly looked over as panic took over my body. Sweat poured from my face and fell onto the hospital gown I was wearing. Renee, my doctor, and two nurses rushed into the room.

My doctor was handsome for a Caucasian man. He resembled Tamera Mowry's husband, Adam. The nurses were speaking so fast and moving about so quickly that I couldn't understand what was going on. I hoped nothing was happening to my baby. Renee stood off to the side and I saw the worry on her face.

"What…what's going on?" I asked through contractions.

"Your baby's heart rate is dropping because it appears the umbilical cord is wrapped around your baby's neck. You're going to be okay, your baby too. We just need you to stay calm," said the nurse.

"How does this happen?" Renee asked.

"Because the fetus moves and kicks inside the uterus, the umbilical cord can wrap and unwrap itself around the baby many times throughout pregnancy. Sometimes the umbilical cord gets stretched and compressed during labor, leading to a brief decrease in blood flow to the fetus. This can cause sudden, short drops in fetal heart rate," replied the nurse.

"We need to prep for a C-section stat," yelled my doctor.

"What? Why?" I cried out in panic.

"The baby is suffering too much distress. We need to get her out. You're going to be okay. Your friend can come back with you if you want," said the nurse.

"I'm definitely going," said Renee.

I couldn't believe what was happening. I'm going to fuck Neron up for having me go through this alone. God please let my baby be okay.

Another nurse rushed back into the room with an anesthesiologist and had me fill out consent forms.

"Ma'am, we just need you to sign off on some consent forms. It won't take long," said the anesthesiologist.

"Shit, what in the hell do I need to sign? Hand me the damn forms," I shouted.

The poor man looked so timid. He swiftly passed me the forms. I didn't read a damn thing. I couldn't concentrate. I hurriedly scribbled my signature. After I was numbed from the waist down, the nurses then quickly gave me a catheter and IV. I watched as the nurses connected heart monitoring equipment to my chest and a blood pressure cuff was placed on my arm. Everything was happening so quickly.

As they wheeled me out of my room, I couldn't believe what I was seeing. Right in front of me was Kimora in a wheelchair with Neron by her damn side! She was getting admitted.

"Neronnnnnnnn! Baby I need you! I have to have a C-section," I yelled through tears as Renee held my hand.

People turned around and stared at me as if I was crazy for calling out to a man who was with another woman in labor, but I didn't care. Kimora turned to me, but was in too much pain to respond. Neron glanced at me and didn't say a word as the nurses wheeled Kimora into a room with Neron trotting behind her. His family and friends shot me looks. Roxy shook her head at me.

"Fuck all y'all for staring at me! Neronnnnnnn! Neron baby I need you," I yelled as I was pushed through two double doors and was on my way to be prepped for surgery, still yelling and calling out for Neron.

"Stop it!" mumbled Renee.

"Don't tell me to stop it. I need him with me," I pleaded.

Renee rolled her eyes. I knew she was embarrassed, but nobody told her to stay with me. Once we made it inside the operating room, a curtain was pulled across my midsection. Renee walked briskly to wash her hands and suited up in a gown and mask. Everything was becoming so real. My senses were out of commission because all I could think about was Neron and my unborn. I couldn't believe he was with Kimora while she was having her baby, yet he chose to ignore me as if I wasn't in labor too *and* needing a C-section.

"Are you okay?" Renee asked.

"Yeah. It's just not fair," I cried.

"Please Gaby, stop it! Just focus on your unborn. You need to relax," she replied with concern.

I took her advice and closed my eyes and took deep breaths.

"You're about to meet your baby," said the doctor. I smiled, excited to meet my daughter.

The incision was made and I couldn't feel a damn thing. "Ms. Hernandez, how are you doing?" The doctor asked.

"I'm fine. I'm ready to meet her," I replied.

"I have to reach my hand underneath the baby's head to form a cradle so I can pull the head out," he said.

Not even two minutes later, my baby was pulled out. I heard her little cry and tears immediately flooded from my eyes. They held her up and she looked just like Neron. She was beautiful.

They whisked her away to get cleaned up and I heard the nurse shout, "She's eight pounds, twelve ounces and twenty-one inches long!"

"What's her name?" One of the nurses asked as she smiled.

"Magdalena Mia Lopez," I said proudly.

"She's beautiful," said the nurse.

"Thank you. She looks just like her daddy," I replied.

Chapter 20

Neron

I had just cut the umbilical cord and couldn't stop staring at my son. He was absolutely beautiful. They quickly placed him on Kimora's chest, not caring that he wasn't clean, she immediately cried as she kissed him. She did great delivering our son. The nurses then took our son to get him cleaned up. I gently kissed Kimora on the lips as I smiled at my woman, the mother of my son.

"You did great baby. I love you so much. Thank you for this precious gift," I said.

"I love you too," she said tiredly.

"I'm going to step right over there and see him. I'll be right back. Is that okay?" I asked.

"Yes baby," she said grinning.

I walked over to the nurses as they were finishing the testing done for newborns. He was doing great! He cried like a grown man when he entered this world. He was my *son!* He looked identical to me. He was seven pounds, eight ounces and twenty-one inches long. We decided to name him a Jr. At that moment, I felt like it wasn't fair that Gabriela was in another room having to go through this alone. Yeah, she got on my damn nerves, but the child was innocent. I had to know if that was my baby. We needed to get this DNA testing done as soon as possible. I didn't want to be one of those people who waited until the child was three or four years old.

The nurses left and let us bond with our son. I sat on the hospital bed as I watched Kimora breastfeed our son. Even after just giving birth, Kimora was still beautiful with her slanted brown eyes, small button nose, butterscotch skin, long curly natural eyelashes and poufy natural hair.

After sitting in the room for about an hour, my parents, Mama Pam, Quan, Kimora's parents and her brother entered our room. Her step mother, Adrienne, decided to stay back out of respect for Roxy. She didn't want to cause any unnecessary tension or drama on such a special and beautiful day. You could see the excitement written all over their faces. Kennard was so thrilled to be an uncle.

"My boy! You're a father now," Quan said walking up to me and giving me daps.

"Yeah man! I have a *son!* It's an amazing feeling brah," I replied.

"Congrats man! I know you'll be great with him. Now, enough of all this sentimental stuff," said Quan smiling and walking off towards Kimora.

Roxy was in tears seeing her daughter become a mom. She placed a vase of beautiful pink roses on the windowpane and sat down on the hospital bed.

"They're beautiful mom," said Kimora admiring the flowers.

"Congratulations Kimora! Welcome to motherhood! Be better than me," Roxy said through tears.

"Thanks mom, that means a lot," she replied with her eyes misty.

"Kimora baby, congrats," said Quan hugging her.

"Thank you bro," she replied smiling.

"Son, let me talk to you," said Kimora's father Dewayne. We walked to the other side of the room. My dad wasn't too far behind us and approached us as well.

"You're responsible for that tiny little life for the rest of your life. He's not a loan. Be there for him. Mentor him. Love him. Show him how to be a man. Only you can do that," said Dewayne as my father nodded.

"Yes sir, you know I am. I wouldn't have it any other way," I replied.

"Sorry to interrupt ya'll," said my mother approaching us. "Now son, I know you got her a *push gift*," said my mom.

"Oh shoot! I did. I almost forgot," I said happy my mom reminded me.

A push gift is a present a father gives to the mother to mark the occasion of her giving birth to their child.

Our parents, Quan, Kennard and Mama P all passed our son around. He was just staring at them probably wondering what the hell was going on. He was so cute.

"Kimora baby," I said, as everyone in the room got quiet. "Thank you for giving me the most precious gift in the world. I know nothing can ever compare to the gift of life, but I wanted to give you this," I said handing her an iPhone six and a pair of 14k white gold diamond stud earrings.

"Wow, thank you, baby," Kimora said cheesing so hard as our parents took pictures. She started crying tears of joy.

"I know you'll be taking lots of photos of Jr. and I figured this would be the best way to do it. I got you the earrings because I know you've been hinting at wanting a pair."

I walked up to her and kissed her gently on the lips. She repeatedly thanked me over and over.

After two hours, everyone left and the nurse came back into the room and asked if we would like him to go to the nursery.

"No thank you. I want him with me," Kimora said.

"It's okay for babies to go to the nursery baby. He will get a bath and you'll be able to get some rest. Take it from me honey, you will never rest again for a few months once you go home with a newborn" said the older woman, smiling. She looked like Jennifer Lewis.

"Um, okay. I could use the rest," replied Kimora. The nurse smiled and gently took the baby from out of Kimora's arms.

Once the nurse left, I sat next to Kimora and wrapped my arm around her neck. She moaned and closed her eyes.

"I'm so tired baby," she said.

"I know baby. Get some rest. I'm going to get this DNA stuff arranged with Gabriela. I'm going to go see the baby," I said, knowing she wasn't going to like this.

"What? You're going to go and see that bitch on our special day that your son was born?" She yelled.

"Calm down, please. Seeing my son being born made me realize that I don't want to wait another second on getting this DNA test done. I don't want to miss out on anything if she is my kid. I couldn't live with myself. Be proud that you have a man that wants to step up and take responsibility," I said, getting off the bed.

Kimora didn't say anything. She looked down at her hands in her lap and exhaled.

"So, you know what you're having? Explain how you know that?" She barked.

"Man, baby, that day she came to the opening, she blurted it out," I replied.

There was silence for a few moments until Kimora spoke.

"Please don't be long. I hate that bitch. I don't want you around her," she responded looking at me.

"Don't worry about her. I don't want her. I'm going to see about this kid. That's it, baby. I love you and only you. You know that," I said, kissing her on the forehead and readjusting her pillows so she could get comfortable.

She smiled.

"I'll be back. Get some rest," I said walking towards the door.

"Okay," she said leaning back onto her pillows and closing her eyes.

*

I'm so glad Kimora didn't give me hell about going to see Gaby and this baby. Deep down, I just wanted to know if this baby was mine. I wanted to be there. Each step I took towards the receptionist desk, I was nervous. On one hand, I didn't want this baby to me mine. On the other hand, I wanted it to be because Gaby was crazy as fuck. I was going to take her to court for full custody if this child was mine.

"Hi. I need Gabriela Hernandez's room number please," I said.

"I need you to sign in and I will get you a nametag," said the bubble gum popping receptionist.

I quickly signed my name, was giving her room number and a nametag. I turned around and walked in the direction of Gaby's hospital room. My heart was beating like Floyd Mayweather's opponent. I was dreading seeing this chick.

I approached her room and stood in front of her room door. I was hesitant on going inside because Gabriela never made anything easy. If it was easy, she made it hard.

I took a deep breath and pushed open her room door. When I walked inside, I saw Gabriela's eyes light up. Her friend stood up and gave me an evil glare.

"What's up? Where's the baby?" I asked getting straight to the point.

"Baby, you came! I knew you wouldn't let me down," she said grinning.

"Where's the baby? We need to get this DNA testing done," I replied.

"You didn't come to check up on me? You only came for the baby?" She asked as if that was a surprise.

"Mannnnn, Gabriela, we're not together. I told you I wanted nothing to do with you until the baby was born and that's only to get this DNA test done," I said glancing at her friend.

"Fuck you Neron! Fuck you," she shouted pulling out her IV.

Her friend stood up and rushed to her side.

"Stop Gaby! Stop this shit," she bellowed.

I stood by the door, staring. I wasn't going anywhere near her crazy ass.

"I'm going to get the nurse, I'll be back," said her friend.

I followed behind her and we both exited the room as Gabriela called out my name.

"The baby is in the nursery if you want to go by and see her. Her name is Magdalena Mia Lopez. I'm Renee by the way," she said.

"Good looking out," I said keeping it short and walking off in the direction of the nursery.

*

I approached the nursery and right in front, was Magdalena. She was cute, but I didn't see any resemblance, compared to my son. I blew air out of my lips and just stared at her as she slept. If she was mine, I wanted both of my kids to know each other. I stood there for ten minutes just watching her and glancing at my son that was near.

I trotted back towards Gaby's room with all kinds of thoughts invading my mind. Once inside, Renee was standing by the bed talking to Gaby. They stopped once they noticed me.

"That's your daughter Neron. You left me to have a C-section alone! You weren't there for me," she cried out.

"Mannnn, you fucked me while I sleep after sneaking into my house. You couldn't possibly believe I was going to be okay with that shit," I replied.

Renee looked crazy when she heard me admit that.

"Y'all niggas will come up with any lie to avoid taking care of your seed," Renee said snickering.

"What chu mean? Yo, you don't even know me. That shit is real. I want this DNA test done. The baby looks nothing like me," I said getting angry.

"Why Neron? Why are you trying me like I'm some hoe? You know that's your baby nigga," Gabriela shouted as she tossed her pillows in my direction. They barely landed near me and fell onto the linoleum floor.

"Gimmie your number. I'm going to call you and we can schedule a day to meet up at the DNA testing center," I said, still standing by the door.

Gabriela looked like I had just proposed to her ass. She quickly spit out her digits as I stored it into my phone. Her contact name was the baby mama from hell.

"I'll call you in a few days. I know you gotta be in here a little longer because of the C-section and I want to give you time to get settled," I said preparing to walk out of the room.

"Neron! Wait! Please, just sit with me for a few minutes. I miss you," she mumbled.

I glanced at her friend, Renee, who looked like she was finally seeing how crazy Gabriela was being. I shook my head and sauntered out of her room, not bothering to give Gaby a reply.

"Neron, please don't go," I heard Gaby repeat loudly over and over as I walked away from her room door.

Chapter 21

Gabriela

I was finally getting discharged from the hospital and was still super sore from the surgery. I was disappointed that Neron hadn't come around. I truly thought this baby would've brought us closer. Thank God for Renee. She had been a great friend during my labor and delivery. She checked in on the boys at home and made sure they got to school, were fed and bathed. She sat with me at the hospital and listened to me weep and vent about Neron.

"Welcome home," Renee said as we pulled into my apartment complex. My three brothers were already standing outside. They couldn't wait to meet their niece. The boys ran towards the car and started helping with the hospital bad and helping me out of the car. Renee grabbed the car seat and we all trotted inside the apartment.

As soon as we walked into the apartment, Magdalena started crying. Her cries immediately irritated me. "Somebody please shut that baby up?" I yelled in frustration.

My brother's smiles turned into frowns. Renee shot me a look. "Uh, boys, how about I put the baby to sleep and I take you guys out for lunch?" Their eyes lit up with excitement. I ignored them and strolled towards my room and locked myself in my bedroom.

I heard Renee giving Magdalena her first little bath because I heard my daughter wailing from being in the water. Tears fell from my face and I couldn't get them to stop. I thought Neron would've been by my side to go through this journey with me, but he's not. He's playing house with Kimora and her baby, but doubting mine. It wasn't fair. My baby didn't deserve this. I didn't deserve this.

I cried myself to sleep and woke up when I heard a knock on my bedroom door. I yawned and sat up. I slowly got out of bed and shuffled towards my bedroom door and unlocked it.

"I bathed the baby, fed her, burped her and changed her. She's asleep. I'm going to take the boys out for a few hours. Try and get some rest," she said. I could tell she was pissed off with me, but she didn't voice her feelings. I guess she was trying to keep the peace between us. I didn't know if I was cut out for motherhood.

*

Eight weeks had passed and I wasn't feeling having a newborn around. She cried all the time. She was colicky and gassy. She never slept for long. She woke up at night, thinking it was morning. I was like a walking zombie. All I wanted to do was sleep.

After the boys left for school and I put the baby down for a nap, I rolled up a blunt and smoked my way into relaxation. "Pass it, baby," said Paul.

We had just finished fuckin' and was sitting on the bed naked and hung the fuck over from clubbing last night. I didn't know how I was able to get the boys up for school, but Jose was a good kid and he helped me. I smirked, thinking about last night.

It was Friday night and I was dog-tired. I didn't want to do shit. I had just fed the baby and the boys were in their room playing a new video game. I didn't want to move. I couldn't do this single parent shit. Yeah, I trapped Neron, but it wasn't fair. I guess you can say things backfired on me.

It was nine pm and I had just put the baby to sleep. I was in flannel pajamas and was watching reruns of Orange

BABY MAMA FROM HELL 2

Is the New Black. Daya was my favorite character. I couldn't wait for season three. I glanced at my phone as it began to ring. I grimaced at Renee's name because I knew why she was calling. All she wanted to do was go out. I wasn't in the mood. I let voice mail take her call. I turned my attention back to the television and heard my phone ringing again. If she called me twice and I didn't answer, she would call again. It was best that I answer her.

"What girl? Damn you know I don't answer the phone while I'm watching Orange Is the New Black, rerun or not," I said laughing, but serious.

People knew not to call me while I was watching Orange Is the New Black or the Walking Dead because I was glued to Darryl's fine redneck ass.

"Come on, bitch! I'm in Pure and Paul is here! Mad bitches are flocking to him." That was all her ass needed to say.

I was very territorial. I was feeling Paul. He was my diversion with his fine ass. So, I did the usual, ordered pizza for the boys, left Jose in charge with ten dollars for an emergency and jetted to the club. I showed up and shut down all those bitches that were flocking to him like a duck to bread. In the end, the best woman won and he came home with me. We wasted no time fucking once we got back to my place. Last night was the first time I'd given my body to him. He took full advantage and I damn sure wasn't complaining.

"I'm so tired of taking care of this baby alone. I fell back a lot on Neron's ass because I'm still adjusting to being a new mom and trying to manage everything, but that fuck nigga hasn't called me at all," I said through puffs.

I was trying to sound as if I hated Neron so I wouldn't run him off. He and I have been kicking it since I had Magdalena. I guess you could say, my heart wanted Neron, but Paul was just a distraction. Yeah I liked him but he wasn't my baby daddy. Neron was Mr. Right and Paul was Mr. Right *Now.* I didn't want Neron with Kimora, so I would do whatever I could in my power to cause friction in their relationship. Call me what you want. Fix your lips. Don't judge me. Love can make you do some crazy things.

"Call him up and demand he take care of his seed," he said taking the blunt from me.

I grabbed my cell phone and decided to call Neron. He was lucky I've been too tired to fuck up his world

BABY MAMA FROM HELL 2

lately. This nigga had another baby and had yet to contact me on this DNA test.

"Hello," he said.

"Neron, it's Kimora," I replied, angrily through the phone.

"What do you want? How did you get this number?" he asked blowing air out of his lips.   Before I could reply, I heard Kimora's annoying voice.

"Who is that?" She asked.

I heard Neron say my name and Kimora instantly went off.

"I'ma fuck you up, bitch! Don't think I'mma let that baby shower incident go unnoticed," I heard her say in the background.

"Tell that trick that she better take some of that bass out of her voice because she's not going to do shit to your baby mama," I shouted back giggling.

Click!

"Did this nigga really just hang up on me?"

Paul shook his head as he got up to relieve himself. He really tried to stay out of Neron's and my business. He only listened to me vent and offered very little advice.

I called back again and again and again. No answer. I decided to try one more time.

"What?" Neron barked into the phone.

"Your damn daughter needs diapers and formula. That's what," I said lying because I still had diapers and formula from the baby shower my coworkers threw for me.

"Mannnnn, I don't know if she's my daughter," he replied, but I could tell he didn't want her to go without the things she needed.

"Don't fuckin' play with me. She *is* your daughter. I'm waiting on your punk ass to get the test done. You're too busy over there playing house and neglecting my baby," I yelled.

I heard him take a deep breath.

"Look, I'll meet you at a gas station, but I'm not doing shit else for you until I get these results. Get on WIC or something because I'm not about to be at your beck and call for a baby that may not be mine," he replied sternly.

"What! Are you fuckin' kidding me, nigga? This is your daughter. We made her and you're going to take care of her whether you want to or not," I shouted as I tightly gripped the phone in my hand.

"I'm not about to fight with you. You're not welcomed at my house and I'm definitely not coming to yours, so meet me at Shell on Beach Boulevard," he said hanging up in my face. I sucked my teeth. I wasn't going to let him keep hanging up on me like that.

"I'll be back baby," I said kissing Paul on his succulent and juicy lips.

"I gotta rise up outta here too," he replied putting on his Hanes boxers. I pouted. I enjoyed his company. I didn't want him to leave.

I tossed on some sweat pants, a wife beater and some old Reeboks. I tied my untamed and messy hair into a bun and placed some ninety-nine cent hair store earrings into my ear. I glanced at myself in the mirror and bags made themselves at home under my eyes. I looked like I felt. Like shit!

I grabbed my sleeping beauty and gently placed her into the car seat. She stirred in her sleep and I froze like a mime. I prayed she stayed sleep. When her eyes fluttered, I crossed my fingers that she would fall back asleep. After a few seconds, she did. I couldn't understand how Neron said she didn't look like him. Magdalena looked just like him. She had my skin tone, but she had his facial features. She was hairy just like him. He was seriously tripping if he couldn't see the resemblance. I smiled at my baby and prayed that I could be the best mother I could to my daughter while still being there for my brothers. It was a lot. Paul grabbed the car seat for me and we left the house together.

"You be safe. I'll call you later," he said hugging me and kissing me on the cheek. He made my legs weak at the knees.

I watched Paul pull off and hoped he could come back later on tonight. I could definitely use another round of his loving. The man was a monster in the bed. I cranked up my car and made my way to my baby daddy, whether he wanted to believe that or not.

*

I pulled up at the Shell gas station and saw Neron putting air into one of his tires. I parked next to him and kept the car running as the AC blew. It was extremely hot today and the sun definitely wanted to be noticed. I couldn't stand the heat. I beeped my horn and Neron turned around and put one finger in the air to signal me to hold on for a moment. I sat staring at him. My heart fluttered. I just couldn't understand how he didn't feel anything for me.

Once he finished putting air into his front tire, he stood up and straightened his T-shirt. He reached into the back seat and pulled out two, one hundred and twenty-eight count, Pampers boxes. I popped my trunk and Neron took the initiative to place the diaper boxes into my trunk. He jogged back towards his car as I noticed his defined and chiseled arms glistening in the sun. The heat was making him perspire, but all it was doing was turning me on. He then grabbed a bag with Gerber Good Start formula inside. He also placed that into the truck. He casually walked around to my side of the car and I rolled my window down. I didn't want him to see the bags under my eyes, so sunglasses decorated my face.

"Thanks for the stuff," I said, trying to be casual for once. I was too tired to fight since I've been getting lack of sleep with a newborn.

"No problem. Look, is tomorrow good for you? I'm ready to get this testing done. I wasn't neglecting you. I was trying to give us both time to get settled into parenthood and find a routine," he said genuinely.

I ran my tongue across my top lip as I watched his mouth move. He was sexy as fuck.

"I wanna fuck you," I blurted out, causing him to stop in mid-sentence.

"Mannnnn, here you go! We not together, Gabriela! If this baby is mine, all we'll be doing is co-parenting. That's if I don't take you to court for full custody," he warned as he leaned against my car.

"Are you kidding me? Take me to court for what?" I shrieked, waking up the baby.

"Man, I'm hearing how you've been clubbing every damn Friday and Saturday. You just had a baby that could possibly be mine. You should be home. Hell, shouldn't you be back at work," he replied standing up straight and folding his arms across his chest.

I can't lie. I have been clubbing with Paul a lot lately, but I deserved some free time and Renee was willing to babysit. Why shouldn't I take her up on the offer to have some free time?

"So what! Don't worry about me and my job. I got this! I had a C-section and needed more maternity time off. I still have a job nigga. Plus, I'm a single parent. I'm the one who took Magdalena to her two-day checkup and six-week checkup. I'm the one getting no sleep or any help," I yelled.

"I ain't got any sympathy for your ass. You brought this shit on yourself trying to pin a baby on me thinking it would bring us back together. I don't know why y'all women think a baby can keep a man. That shit does nothing but complicate things. Your plan failed and Kimora and I are still together. Grow the fuck up," he said walking off towards his car.

His words stung me like a wasp. A tear slid down my cheek as my daughter cried that I wasn't picking her up right away. Anger filled my body as I floored the gas pedal and drove in Neron's direction. He hurriedly jumped in his car as I drove passed him. I wasn't going to hit him, but I wanted to scare him and I did just that.

Fuck him!

189

Chapter 22

Neron

Every time I tried to be cordial to this woman, she made me regret it. I couldn't stand Gabriela's thirsty ass. I drove home pissed off. I had to lie to Kimora and tell her that I was running to the Barbershop to pop up on my employees and see how things were doing. It wasn't a total lie because I was going to drop by the barbershop, but I failed to mention that I was meeting Gabriela first. I just didn't want to hear Kimora's mouth.

I drove to my barbershop with Gabriela on my mind. We needed to get this DNA test done. I glanced at Magdalena in the back seat when I was talking to her mother earlier and no doubt she was a cute little girl, but she just didn't look like me.

I grabbed my cell phone that was resting on my console and dialed Gaby's number. There was no use in blocking my number anymore since her crazy behind had it already. I shook my head thinking about how sneaky Gaby was. She could work for the CIA or secret service.

"What?" She barked into the phone.

"Gurl, kill all that shit. You just tried to run me over. Fuck you got an attitude for?" I replied raising my voice.

"I'm sorry. I wasn't going to hit you. I just wanted to scare you," she said lowering her voice.

"You wild man. That shit ain't cool. I swear you be trying the shit outta me and one day you gonna push the wrong button and I'ma lay you out," I said irritated.

"Whatever Neron. You're definitely not about that life," she replied, snickering into the receiver.

There was no use going back and forth with her. I just needed to tell her something.

"Look tomorrow, we have an appointment to get this DNA test done. I was trying to tell your loopy ass the time and location before you went berserk. You need to be there *with* the baby at eleven o'clock. I'm paying for everything," I said, turning into my business.

"I can't believe you doubt Magdalena, Neron. How can you not see the resemblance?" She asked.

"Cut all that out. I don't trust you. Hell, I don't trust anyone that would break into their ex's house and fuck them to make a baby," I added, getting pissed off.

There was silence.

"Gaby, I know you hear me. Be there tomorrow at eleven," I repeated.

"I'll be there. I want an apology when the test comes back that she's your daughter," she countered.

"Nah, never that. The only thing that will change is that I will be in my daughter's life. That's it. Look, I gotta go. I'll see you tomorrow," I said cutting off my car.

"Okay. I love you," she replied.

I rolled my eyes. This chick just didn't get it.

"Goodbye Gabriela," I said hanging up on her.

I closed my car door and stood in front of my barbershop, admiring my company. Business was booming and the money was coming in great. There was no doubt that I could take care of another baby if Magdalena were mine. Tomorrow was the day.

*

"Neron, it's your turn," I heard Kimora mumble in her sleep. Our son was crying and it was my turn to feed and change him.

"I got him, baby," I murmured as I sat up and wiped the sleep out of my eyes. I swung my feet over the bed and yawned.

"Okay lil man, daddy's here," I said picking up my son. He was growing into his looks and had a head full of curly hair. He had my complexion and Kimora's family trait of long twisted eyelashes.

I warmed up some breast milk and proceeded to change him. I looked at the clock on our dresser and it was almost nine in the morning. Gabriela better have had her ass ready for this DNA appointment.

After I fed and changed my son, he was soon fast asleep and snoring. What eight-week-old baby snored? My son, that's who! He definitely was my seed. I smiled as I watched him sleep. The sound of my cell phone vibrating diverted my attention from him. I kept it on silent since the baby was sleeping in our room in his bassinet. Kimora wasn't ready for him to start sleeping in his nursery.

Before I could answer, Kimora, who had gone to the restroom, answered. I already knew it was about to be some shit.

"What bitch?" Kimora asked. She was straight to the point as she exited our bedroom, careful not to wake our sleeping son.

"Well, good morning to you boo," I heard Gaby reply loudly into the phone.

"Nah, bitch you don't deserve no greeting you THOT! What do you want with *my* man?"

"Put *our* baby daddy on the phone hoe. I don't owe you any explanation," I heard her say.

I quickly snatched the phone from Kimora because I knew my baby's patience. She was about to flip.

"What Gabriela?" I asked, annoyed.

I put the phone on speakerphone so Kimora could be included. I ain't have time for Kimora to start tripping on me, thinking I was secretive or some shit.

"My car has a flat tire. I need a ride to the DNA appointment unless you want to reschedule," she said.

She knew what she was doing. I shook my head as I looked at Kimora. She was pissed.

"Look, I'll come and get you. Be ready," I said hanging up.

Kimora stomped off towards the kitchen and started making a pot of coffee.

"Baby, just hear me out," I said.

"Hear what out? That crazy, psycho, delusional ass bitch wants you and you're falling for her every move," she replied, slamming a coffee mug down on the granite top counter.

"First off, I'm not falling for anything. I just want to see if this child is mine. If I have to give her a ride, so be it. You need to trust me," I said walking up on her to her and grabbing her chin.

She sucked her teeth.

"Look, too many men in this world let a crazy chick like Gabriela run them away from being a part of a child's life or doing something simple as taking a DNA test. I'm not that type of man. I'm having the results sent to me, so after today I won't have to deal with her anymore if the child isn't mine. If she is, I'll be taking her to court. I'm just trying to do the right thing," I replied kissing her softly on the lips.

"I love you Kimora and only you. Always have," I said kissing her again.

"I love you too," she replied, giving in.

I placed Kimora on the countertop and opened her fluffy, plum robe. Her trimmed Kit Kat stared back at me. I slipped two fingers inside her and quickly located her G-spot like MapQuest as I curled my fingers in a come-hither motion. I went to work as if I was trying to stroke her belly button from inside her.

"You like that baby?" I asked watching her mouth form the letter O.

Satisfied with the way Kimora had her eyes rolling into the back of her head, and lack of response to my question, I smiled. I pulled out my fingers that were now coated with her sweet, sugary juices and stuck my two fingers inside Kimora's mouth. She sucked them clean.

"Neronnnnn, the coffee," she said squirming.

"Nah, you'll get your coffee once you feed your man breakfast," I replied as I dived in like I was on a slip and slide and went to work with my tongue.

Kimora was too busy moaning that I don't think she heard a thing I said.

"Yessssssss," yelled Kimora as she spread her legs further apart giving me more access.

"I'm coming!!" She whimpered, fidgeting around. She grabbed the cabinet knobs on each side of her and flung them open as she held on for dear life as she rode her Orgasm into town.

I stepped back and laughed at the sight before me. Kimora sat there still holding onto the kitchen cabinet knobs, panting, trying to catch her breath. I walked towards her and helped her down from the countertop. To my shock, Kimora dropped to her knees and pulled down my boxers. She wrapped her right hand around the base of my meat and stuffed me into her mouth. Kimora could suck a golf ball through a garden hose. Her mouth skills couldn't be duplicated. My knees buckled and I felt like I was going to pass out. She was sucking the life out of me.

"Damn gurl," I said with my eyes closed as I tugged on her hair.

She pulled my member out of her mouth and started to jack me up and down, as she looked me directly in the eyes.

"I want to remind you of what you have a baby," she said before she stuffed me back into her mouth and went to work.

Damn, I was like putty in her hands right now. If she kept this up, I would be the one rescheduling this DNA appointment.

Chapter 23

Gabriela

I was up bright and early, excited to see Neron. I shipped the boys off to school and tidied up my place. I had just finished washing my hair when a brilliant idea popped into my head. I wrapped a towel around my wet hair and ran towards my closet. I pulled out my utility blade and trotted outside to my car and slashed my passenger rear tire. I watched as the tire slowly deflated and smiled. I walked back into the house and called Neron.

Kimora was a thorn in my side. I hated her ass. She was going to have to get used to me being around because I had another kid by him. That killed her. I know she wasn't too thrilled about me getting a ride from her man. I was going to seduce him like no other. Now y'all can say I'm crazy and whatever. I don't care. I love that man. I will do whatever to make him see that I'm the one for him. Kimora was just temporary.

I just finished curling my hair and tossing on some hip hugging jeans when my doorbell rang. The sound startled Magdalena and she woke up, fluttering her eyes and whining, wanting me to pick her up. I ignored

Magdalena and walked briskly towards the door and flung it open without looking out the peephole. There stood Neron with his hands stuffed in his jeans with a serious look on his face.

"You ready?" He asked, not moving or attempting to walk into my apartment.

"Yeah, I just have to grab my stuff and we can be out. Come inside," I said walking off.

"Nah, I'm good. Just pass me the baby and I can strap her inside the car and will wait for you in the car," he replied.

I sucked my teeth. "I don't bite Neron," I said turning around and smiling at him seductively as I grabbed the baby and put her into her car seat.

Neron didn't respond as he took the baby from me and walked off in the direction of his car. I shook my head. *This is going to be harder than I thought.* I grabbed my belongings and walked outside. The bright sun beamed down on my face. I tossed on my sunglasses to protect my eyes. *I hate this heat.*

I made it to Neron's car and saw him turning around and looking at Magdalena and making silly faces. I smiled seeing him interact with her. I slipped into the passenger seat and placed a pacifier into Magdalena's mouth and strapped on my seatbelt.

"You look good *baby daddy*," I said eyeing him.

He had just got a fresh tape up and smelled all good. I smiled when I looked down and saw his dick print through his pants. Damn, I missed that shit, but he was definitely not feeling me right now because my comment made his jaw tighten. He really was uncomfortable around me. I didn't know why.

"I guess you've been in my closet because we're matching," I said trying to lighten the tension in the car. We both were sporting blue jeans with a red shirt.

He didn't respond. He just kept his eyes on the road. He didn't even have any music on.

"Neron? Why are you giving me the silent treatment?" I asked dumbfounded.

"Gaby, man, is you really that clueless? You just tried to run me over yesterday! You tried to ruin the grand opening of my barbershop, you crashed Kimora's baby shower, you've drugged Kimora, you had her arrested, and you broke into our home and then fucked me! Now I might have another baby with your ass. I don't fuck with you. It's hard for me to even be this close to you without wanting me to choke your ass out," he said as calm as he could muster up.

I sat quietly and took in his words.

"I only did those things because I love you," I replied turning my body to look at him.

"Well, I don't love you," he replied matter-of-factly as we pulled up to the DNA testing center. His words broke my heart. A tear slipped from my cheek as Neron hopped out of the car and picked up the baby. I followed behind him as we went inside and checked in.

While Neron signed us in, I sat down and twiddled my thumbs. I hated rejection. I've been rejected my whole life. I was sick of it. I smirked watching Magdalena smile in her sleep. I was going to love her and give her the best life I could. I wanted to make things work with Neron even more now that she was here.

Neron sat down across the room and scrolled through his phone. I know he was probably texting Kimora. I shook my head. Within ten minutes, Neron's last name was called. He walked towards me and picked up the baby carrier and we all trotted in the back. The process was quick as Neron and Magdalena got the insides of their cheeks swabbed. Neron put a rush on the test and we were going to have the results in a few days.

After leaving the DNA testing center, I sat in the back of the car and fed Magdalena a bottle. She was really fussy and cranky and she was putting my plans on hold that I had for seducing Neron. Neron said not one word the entire drive back to my place.

We pulled up to my apartments and he helped carry Magdalena to the front door. I had to think of something quick because I didn't want him to leave me just yet.

"Neron!" I yelled as he was descending the stairs.

"What?" He barked.

"Um, do you mind putting the spare on my car, please?" I begged, pouting.

"Find somebody else to do it," he shot back.

"Neron, I have nobody else to ask," I said sadly. *Damn, I couldn't even get him to change my tire when he used to wait on me hand and foot when I was pregnant with Mia.*

"Where's your keys?" he asked turning around and walking back up the stairs. I smiled on the inside. I hurried and unlocked the front door and passed Neron my car keys. Magdalena was knocked out so I left her in her car seat and sat it on the floor by the couch. As I was preparing to walk out the front door, my cell phone rang and Renee's name flashed across the screen.

"Hello," I said answering.

"Yasssss, murder this pussy!" I heard Renee moaning.

I took the phone from my ear and scrunched up my face. I know that bitch didn't just call me to prove that she was getting some dick. I put the phone back to my ear and was about to hang up when I heard a familiar voice.

Nah, this can't be happening. As I was about to reply, the call disconnected. I was shaking. I squeezed the phone so hard that I was sure it was going to crack. I wiped the beads of sweat from my forehead and decided to deal with that shit later. Right now, I needed to try and seduce Neron and get him in my bed, but best believe, I was about to show up and show out on Renee.

That bitch swore she was my friend though! Tried to tell me to stay to myself at the job because all the females did was gossip and hate. Now, I see why she said that because she was a hoe! She was dick crazy and scandalous and was probably fucking all the females' men from the job. How dare she fuck Paul knowing I was feeling that man! Why would he do that? Why was it okay for these bitches to keep stealing my man?

I swallowed a lump in my throat and pushed Renee and Paul to the back of my mind. I'll definitely deal with that later. I ran outside to see Neron jacking up my car, preparing to put on my spare tire. He looked so damn good. I walked up to him and tried to pass him a bottle of cold water.

"No thank you," he replied.

I sat the water on top of the car and started to massage his shoulders. He jerked away from me and stood up.

"You bitch," I heard.

I turned around and saw Kimora running towards me from her car. I guess that bitch was watching us the entire time and I didn't notice. I didn't have a chance to react when she punched me dead in the face. I charged at her and we tussled, pulling hair and cursing at each other.

"You stupid bitch! I trust Neron, I don't trust you," said Kimora, who was now swinging wildly at my face.

I was eating those hits though. I tried my best to fight back, but she was like a wild Pit-bull. I managed to hit her a few times, but nothing compared to the ass whopping she was serving me.

I saw Neron standing there watching the fight as if he was enjoying it.

"Get her off me!" I yelled. He slowly walked towards me as if he'd seen enough and attempted to break us up, but Kimora had a lock of my hair and began dragging me across the hot pavement. I felt the skin on my knees being ripped open. I tried to grab whatever I could on her body to fight back, but it was no use. She had whooped my ass again.

"Bitch, I had written an IOU on that ass bitch! I told you I was coming for you. You up here trying to seduce my man bitch. Yeah, Neron knew I was following y'all because I know you. You're a sneaky bitch," She roared. I felt blood trickling down my chin and touched my face. It was coming from my nose.

I felt someone pull me off the ground as Neron pulled Kimora back, finally separating us. Neighbors had come outside to be nosey and probably got a good show. My knees were bleeding and some of my hair was scattered across the parking lot. This bitch had pulled out some of my real hair.

"What the fuck are y'all doing?" Yelled my ex-neighbor, Ryan.

Ryan was a cutie though. Everyone compared him to the singer August Alsina.

"Mannnn, this doesn't concern you," Kimora fired back.

"Yes, it does concern me. She just gave birth to my daughter almost eight weeks ago," he responded, looking confused at everyone.

The color drained from my face and I just wanted to disappear. Why the fuck did this nigga have to show up, especially without contacting me first.

"What the fuck is he talking about Gabriela? Is this shit true?" roared Neron.

Oh, shit!

About the Author

Born in Louisville Kentucky, Rikenya had always had a passion for writing. She kept a journal from eighth grade until she turned twenty-one years old. She would write faithfully every night before bed. Now at the age of twenty-six, she resides in Jacksonville Florida with her high school sweetheart and is a mother of two daughters, sixteen months apart. She's currently working on new material and working towards her bachelor's degree in Business Administration.

Thank you for the support!

Please leave a review!

To Interact With The Author:

Personal Facebook Page: Facebook.com/Rikenya

Instagram.com/RikenyaXoXo

Twitter.com/RikenyaXoXo

Goodreads Author Page: Goodreads.com

Facebook Fan Page: Facebook.com

Other Available Titles:

Unlucky In Love

Hustle Hard

Money Make Me Come

Baby Mama From Hell

CPSIA information can be obtained
at www.ICGtesting.com
Printed in the USA
LVHW080038100722
723114LV00014B/861

9 781514 316566